Demon in the Rift
Stacy Rae

Book Cover by Stacy Rae

Illustrations by Stacy Rae

Page Edges and Chapter Page Image by Painted Wings Publishing Services

First Edition 2025

Paperback ISBN: 979-8-9918153-2-1

E-book ISBN: 979-8-9918153-3-8

Dedication

This book in The Green Witch Project is dedicated to my aunt Mel. She passed away unexpectedly on January 6, 2025. She was always one of my go-to people when I was unsure of a scene. She was so excited when she found out the shop—her character in my book owned—would be on the cover. She got to pick out the colors and the font on the front window of the shop. I just wish she were here to read *Demon in the Rift*. She would be so excited with her character's accomplishments in this one.

You are truly loved and missed.

Blurbs

"Sadie Craig and Izzy Monroe are back—alongside their shape-shifting, magically bound boyfriends, Luca and Colin—navigating the hidden world of magic lurking beneath Salem's surface. But this time, protecting the dangerous spell book they've been entrusted with means confronting a deadly force from another realm: the same demon who murdered their grandparents." Amanda K., Line Editor, Red Adept Editing

"Fledgling witches Izzy and Sadie are forced to take a crash course in using their newfound elemental powers when a dangerous demonic foe threatens to wreak havoc on their dimension. With the help of their familiars, Colin and Luca, and the backing of the Green Witch Project, Izzy and Sadie fight to protect everything that's dear to them. Fans of this paranormal series will relish every twist and turn in Demon in the Rift." Brittany M., Proofreader, Red Adept Editing

Contents

Prologue   XI

Chapter One   1

Chapter Two   5

Chapter Three   15

Chapter Four   21

Chapter Five   29

Chapter Six   35

Chapter Seven   43

Chapter Eight   49

Chapter Nine   53

Chapter Ten   59

Chapter Eleven   67

Chapter Twelve   73

Chapter Thirteen   77

Chapter Fourteen   83

Chapter Fifteen   89

Chapter Sixteen 95

Chapter Seventeen 105

Chapter Eighteen 115

Chapter Nineteen 129

Chapter Twenty 139

Chapter Twenty-One 143

Chapter Twenty-Two 149

Chapter Twenty-Three 153

Chapter Twenty-Four 161

Chapter Twenty-Five 167

Chapter Twenty-Six 169

Chapter Twenty-Seven 175

Chapter Twenty-Eight 181

Chapter Twenty-Nine 189

Chapter Thirty 195

Chapter Thirty-One 199

Chapter Thirty-Two 205

Chapter Thirty-Three 219

Chapter Thirty-Four 225

Acknowledgments 227

About the Author 229

Prologue
Friday, June 23, 2023

Izzy

Dear Diary,

These past five weeks have been an emotional roller coaster. Pops was killed the day I got to town. When our parents arrived, they told me and Sadie that we're cousins—not just close family friends like we'd grown up believing. My mom and her dad are brother and sister, and Pops is my actual grandfather. That was a bittersweet revelation for me since it feels like I missed out on so many opportunities with him and now it's too late.

Our parents said that we have paranormal powers and that Pops did too. Now we have to guard an evil spell book that Pops had been watching over. Our parents can't protect it because they don't have paranormal powers. The gift skipped their generation.

Our Grams, who passed away from a car accident a couple of years before we were born, was actually run off the road and killed by the same man that members of the Green Witch Project think killed Pops. The Green Witch Project is some kind of covenant that deals in paranormal activity and security systems. Our parents work for them as well. They also go by the name Greater World Protection for the security systems side of things. Paranormals and those who know about the paranormal world watch for paranormal activity and deal with any potential threats. I'm still trying to figure out all the things that they do, but that's the gist of it.

Pops sent us a coded letter and left us his journals and diary, and we performed the transference spell in there that allowed us to absorb Pops's energies from his black onyx ring. We didn't really notice anything different afterward, so we aren't sure what it does exactly.

Pops gifted us two cat familiars for us to bind to. I was very hesitant at first because I didn't want to be forced to bind to someone since the connection is supposed to be stronger than marriage—even though we had a reversal spell. After spending time with him, he proved to me that he was trustworthy and an amazing teacher. Of course, I fell head over heels for him, too, and now, I am bound to Colin, a blond-haired, icy-blue-eyed man who goes by the name Smokey when he's in his gray Burmese cat familiar form. Sadie bound herself to Luca, a black-haired, light-gray-eyed man who is a Bombay cat in his familiar form and goes by the name Binx. We can communicate telepathically with the one we are bound to, which was very startling when I wasn't expecting it. They have been very helpful, keeping us grounded in this new situation.

We went up against a warlock tonight. He was the same one who knocked me into a pillar at the cemetery while I was there visiting

Pops. I never should have gone off on my own that night, especially after the warlock broke into our house. But Sadie and I got into a fight because she did the binding spell with Luca after only a few days of knowing him, and she didn't tell me about it. Now, after deciding to bind myself to Colin and everything that's happened since, I can admit I may have overreacted.

Oh, yeah. We inherited Pops's house and his shop, Roots & Remedies.

It has been a whirlwind of change around here. Tomorrow is the grand reopening of the shop. I'm excited, sad, and nervous about running it, but since our parents are close by in Salem now, I know they will help when they can.

Good night,

Izzy

P.S. We are also taking off a semester so we can get used to this new life. Thankfully, when we go back to school, it will all be online.

Chapter One
Saturday, June 24, 2023

Sadie

Neva, Luca, Colin, Izzy, and I stood looking at the blank piece of paper that Celeste Bane, the leader of the Green Witch Project, had given me from Pops. It was supposed to reveal where he'd hidden Hazel Craig's spell book.

We had just closed up after the grand reopening of our shop, Roots & Remedies, which we had inherited after Pops's death last month. Celeste had stopped in to update us on what information the GWP had been able to retrieve from Warrick the warlock. According to Warrick, someone else was supposed to make contact during our grand reopening, but no one had stood out.

I gently nudged Izzy. "Are you guys ready?"

"Yeah, in three, two, one..." Izzy said.

"Seen by you, but not by me.
Ever hidden from my view,

long I'll seek, and find I will.
Now I see it, but they still don't."

Within ten seconds, the page's ink turned visible, and the five of us stood staring at the paper. In small writing, rows upon rows of numbers separated by dashes and commas covered the front and back of the paper. Pops had left us another puzzle.

I stared at the writing for a few moments then turned to Izzy. "Are these like the codes we did with Pops, where we had to use books to decode them?"

Izzy nodded. "Yeah, I think so. The first number should be the page, then the line number, then the word. The final number should be the letter within that word. But it doesn't say which book will break the code."

"Maybe it's one of the books Pops always read to us at night." I glanced at Neva, who was all smiles and had her hands folded in front of her. "Why are you looking at me like that?"

She chuckled. "It seems Raymond had been training you two since you were small for this very moment."

I tilted my head and glanced back down at the paper. "Yeah, I guess so. I just wish we had known about this life when we were little."

Neva placed her hand on my arm. "I'm sure Raymond wished he could have told you more too."

I handed Luca the paper, and he looked over the code. "Do you have any idea what book this would work with?"

I raised my brows and shook my head. "I have no clue. We have the entire series of Goosebumps books and some of the Nancy Drew series and quite a few others mixed in. I'm thinking it's gotta be one of our books since the highest page number is one hundred sixty-seven."

Izzy leaned forward, placing her elbows on the countertop at the kitchen island and resting her chin in her hands. "Doesn't Pops have a bunch of small spell books and cookbooks in his office too?"

"Oh gosh. He does. He didn't teach us how to figure out which book it is, though. This might take a while." I scratched the side of my head.

Colin slid the notebook of customer remedy requests to the middle of the island. "Why don't we start on the code later? Right now, we can help you get some of these requests out of the way."

Izzy ripped out a clean sheet of paper and pushed the notebook in front of me. "Read off the ones you know how to make, and we can start with those."

Twelve requests were listed, and I knew how to make seven of them. The rest I would have to look up in Pops's journals. "Fire cider, rash paste, purification kits, white sage smudge, a protection jar, and relaxation salve. I'll start with these. I'm short on herbs for one of them, and the other five, I've never made." I took a deep breath and slowly released it. "I guess I'll start pulling the herbs."

Luca leaned down and kissed the top of my head before I slid off the barstool.

"I'll be right behind you," he said.

I gave him a quick nod and headed toward the front room, where I stored my herbs behind my desk. As I walked through the doorway, though, I stopped dead in my tracks to stare out the shop's front window. I backed up slowly, bumping into Luca. Gasping, I turned to him and leaned my forehead against his chest.

"Sadie! What's wrong?" He pushed my shoulders back to search my face.

I lifted my chin to meet his eyes. "The guy I saw with Pops on the day I got to Salem was just peering in the window."

Chapter Two

Saturday, June 24, 2023

Sadie

Luca and Colin ran to the front door and out onto Main Street. They stood for a moment, looking around before Luca came back inside.

"Did you see which way he went?" he asked.

I shook my head, and he turned to walk out again but stopped.

"Lock all the doors, and don't open them for anyone but us or Sheriff Veron."

I nodded quickly and locked the door behind him. He and Colin ran down Main Street in different directions. Luca was pulling his phone out to call someone. I ran back into the kitchen, and Izzy was already locking the door there.

Neva looked at us. "Come stay away from the view of the front door." She turned the lights off.

We all leaned against the cabinets, and I started feeling shaky, so I slid down to sit on the floor. Izzy and Neva sat with me.

Neva reached out and grabbed both of our hands. "The guys will call Sheriff Veron and let him know what's going on. He will probably be here shortly after they search for that man."

I tried my best to hold back the tears threatening to escape my eyes and glanced at Izzy. "Did you see him?"

She shook her head. "No. I was at the sink when you saw him."

I took a deep breath. "I saw his eyes. They were solid black. Just like Pops said they were in his journal."

Neva laid her hand on my shoulder. "Black eyes? Are you sure they weren't just dark?"

I shook my head. "No, they were solid black."

Neva rubbed her eyes. "This doesn't make any sense. Only demons have eyes like that. They can't get in our realm, though."

A bag of lavender fell out of the cabinet and spilled on the counter beside the sink. I stood up to close the cabinet door and looked down at the herbs as they moved on their own. After about ten seconds, the herbs lay in the shape of a W.

"Pops? Is that you?"

Izzy glanced at me as she and Neva both stared down at the counter. A message was forming in the herbs. After about a minute, it read, *We were wrong.*

"We were wrong about what?" I looked at Neva.

Neva pulled out her phone. "Did anyone else know about his eyes?"

I shook my head. "I don't know. Veron said that Mavis saw his face, but he didn't say anything about black eyes."

She gave me a quick nod, pushed a couple of buttons on her phone, and put it up to her ear. "Celeste, it's Neva. We have a huge problem. I'm here with the girls. I think we've been searching in the wrong place for Raymond's killer. Sadie saw his eyes. They are solid black." She was quiet for a moment. "I know, but Raymond spelled out 'we were wrong' in some spilled herbs when Sadie mentioned his eyes. Luca and Colin just went after him." She was quiet again. "I'll let you know if he communicates with us again." She hung up and slid her phone back into her pocket.

When she glanced at me, I shot her a confused look. "What does his eye color have to do with anything?"

Neva released a big sigh. "If his eyes are truly black, then that means we are dealing with a much more powerful force than we first thought."

Izzy sought Neva with her eyes. "As in what type of force? How did they get into our realm?"

Neva grabbed our hands again. "I'm not sure, but it seems like we have been looking in the wrong place since your grandmother Rosie was murdered."

I scanned the room then focused on the herbs scattered across the counter, no longer spelling anything. "Pops. Do you know how they got here?"

The herbs started moving slowly again, leaving random letters that didn't spell anything yet, then my phone beeped. I pulled it from my pocket and read the notification. "It's Luca. They are at the front door."

Neva nodded. "You two stay here. I'll let them in."

She walked to the front door, and I could hear Luca ask her where we were.

Luca and Colin came into the kitchen and stood behind us as we watched the herbs forming words. They stopped moving after another minute had passed.

"Um. Pops? Are you still there?" I stared at the words.

Luca leaned closer. "He might not have enough energy to finish the message, but I think I know what he's trying to tell us."

"How does 'rift ley lin x' make any sense to you? I'm so confused."

He moved the spilled herbs, adding an E to the end of *lin*. "I think he's trying to tell us that a rift is opening where the ley lines cross."

My brows furrowed in confusion. "Ley lines? Why would a rift open where they cross?"

Neva backed away from the counter and went to sit at the island. "It's said that wherever ley lines cross, that spot holds vortex-type power. I would assume a rift could open anywhere at those points. Some stories even claim people have disappeared off the face of the earth while studying them."

Someone knocked at the front door, and Luca went to answer it. When he returned to the kitchen a minute later, Veron followed.

I gave him a quick nod. "Did you find him?"

Veron shook his head and looked at Neva. "Celeste called and told me about his eyes. Luca thinks he might know who it is."

I spun around from cleaning up the herbs. "Who is it?"

Luca walked me to the stool so I could sit down, and Colin pulled Izzy around to sit beside me.

Then Luca released a big sigh. "Do you remember when we told you about being tortured in that other realm?"

Izzy and I nodded.

"We were pulled into that realm about three months after we met Raymond. The guy refused to tell us who he wanted us to kill unless we agreed to do it, but now I'm thinking he wanted us to kill Raymond. That guy's eyes were jet-black. Raymond pulled us back to this realm before the guy told us anything about it. The questions he asked me make sense now, though. He was digging for the spell book's location."

Neva came closer to us. "You didn't tell him, did you?"

Luca shook his head. "I couldn't. I didn't know. I still don't know where it is. I won't find out until Sadie and Izzy do, if they choose to tell us."

Neva gave him a little nod. "Few know its location."

Luca shook his head. "If this demon is the same one who killed Raymond and Rosie, then why did he wait so long after killing Rosie to try again? But it makes sense why no one saw him leave that day. That realm has different types of powers. He tried offering me all kinds of new abilities, one of which was invisibility."

My eyes grew wide. "Oh, that's just great. Does the GWP have something to stunt his power so he can't use that?"

Luca shook his head. "Not that I know of. As far as we know, no one in this realm has that kind of power. We just have the invisibility cloak, which doesn't make you completely invisible."

I slid down from the stool. "What can we do to help?"

Luca held out his hand to stop me and gave me a stern gaze. "You can't. You haven't even started elemental training. You and Izzy aren't leaving our sides until he's caught."

I got back up on the stool. "Veron, did Mavis say anything about his eyes that day you spoke to her?"

Veron shook his head. "Yes and no. She said he wore a hat and that his eyes looked dark, but she didn't mention anything about them being black."Luca tilted his head at Veron. "The guy I met didn't constantly have black eyes until his intentions turned bad. When he spoke to one of his minions, his eyes were dark gray."

Veron jotted notes in his journal then glanced up at us and back at Luca and Colin. "Take the girls back to the house. It's already been cleared, so it's safe to go there. James, Barnes, and Carson are already there to stand watch." He looked at Neva. "Since he could have seen you here with the girls, I'm sending Cyrus to stand watch at your house. The others will be right around the corner if he needs them."

She gave him a quick nod, and he turned his attention to us. "Stay with Luca and Colin. Don't go anywhere by yourselves until I call to tell you otherwise. Finding him is now top priority with the GWP. Let us know if Raymond communicates any more information."

Luca looked over at us. "Pack up what you can to finish your customer orders. I'll go get the car."

Veron clicked the button on his radio. "Kingston, Davis, can you come down to the back of Roots & Remedies on Main Street for a police escort?"

The radio beeped, and someone on the other end said, "Ten-four," before it cut back out.

He looked at us. "Kingston and Davis will drive you all home. They should be here within the next ten minutes."

Luca glanced at me. "What all do you need to work on tonight?"

Colin went into the front room with Izzy to help her pack what she needed. I gathered what I needed for the requests that had been made at the grand opening earlier and collected my laptop and cord.

"Can you and Colin bring in the wagon that is in the greenhouse?" I asked Luca as he walked over to the kitchen door. "I don't want to leave Neva's products out there."

He gave me a quick nod, and they went outside to grab it. I emptied a box that held a couple of empty jars and started putting my supplies into it. Izzy came back into the kitchen with her tray of beads and wires.

"Do you have everything you need?" I asked.

She gave me a half smile and raised her eyebrow. "I think so."

I turned to Neva. "Do you wanna stay at our house for a little while?"

She shook her head. "I'll be okay. I've gotta get home to Simba. He doesn't like being by himself for too long. Please call me if you need me or if something happens. I'll come right over."

I hugged her. "Thank you so much. I'm sorry for dragging you into all this."She gave a little giggle. "You're forgetting I signed up for this. This isn't my first rodeo."

Someone knocked at the greenhouse door, and Luca went to open it.

"Our escorts are here." His eyes shifted to Neva. "Do you need one of us to ride with you?"

She patted his arm and winked. "That's very sweet, but I'll be okay."

She headed out the door with an officer, and we followed her out to the second police car.

We got home a few minutes later and locked the doors as soon as we got inside. Colin headed to the kitchen to put a couple of pizzas in the oven. We sat on the couch, and I started tying the white sage for the smudge wraps.

Izzy grabbed my hand. "Are you okay? You're shaking so bad."

A tear that I had been trying to hold back snuck down my cheek. "No. That man is a monster. I have no clue how to stop him from coming after us."

Luca sat beside me on the couch and pulled me close. "You have us as well as the entire GWP to keep you safe."

I wiped another tear that fell down my cheek. "Look how that worked out for Pops."

Izzy rubbed the back of my hand. "Pops didn't tell anyone about his encounter. If he had, he would still be with us."

"If that man is a demon, how did he not set off any of the sensors the GWP has everywhere?" I glanced from Luca to Colin.

Luca pulled me a bit closer. "If we had known he could cross into our realm, we would have had his energy signature in the system, and it would have set off the sensors. But since we have never encountered a demon in our realm, there was no way to know."

Izzy dropped my hand and slid over so Colin could sit beside her. "I'm sure Dad and Elliott are working on something already. We just need to keep our eyes open at all times."

A couple of hours later, Luca walked back to the bedroom with me, and I got my pajamas and went to the bathroom. Once I was in bed and covered up, he leaned down and kissed the top of my head. "I'll be right outside in the living room if you need me."

I gave him my puppy dog eyes. "Will you stay in here with me tonight?"

He let out a little chuckle and pulled out his phone. "Yeah, I'll text Colin and let him know." He pushed some buttons on his phone, and it beeped a few seconds later. He stepped back from the bed as his green spiritual cloud wrapped around his body, and Binx in his feline form jumped onto the bed to snuggle up beside me. He put his paw on my hand, and I closed my hand around it. I was asleep a few moments later.

Chapter Three
Sunday, June 25, 2023

Izzy

I woke to find Smokey curled against my side and gave him a quick scratch on his cheek.

He lay there for a few moments before he stretched and yawned. "*Good morning, sunshine.*"

His voice in my head caught me off guard, and I jumped. "Good morning. Am I ever going to get used to hearing you in my head?"

He got up and stretched again then sat down. "*Maybe one day.*"

I kissed the top of his head and climbed out of bed. Walking to my bedroom door, I opened it and glanced back at him. He tilted his head.

"Come on. I've gotta get dressed."

He jumped down from the bed and stretched his back legs before he meandered to the door.

"Sometime today, Mister Pokey Cat."

He finally made it out into the hall, and I shut the door then rolled my eyes and giggled. I grabbed my old Care Bears T-shirt and a pair of cotton shorts and got dressed, then headed out to the living room to sit on the couch beside Colin. "What do you want to eat this morning?"

He shrugged. "I'm not sure. Have you ordered groceries yet?"

I looked toward the kitchen then back at him. "Oh crap, no. I think it's on my to-do list. I don't even know what we have."

Someone knocked at the door, and I jumped. Colin went to open it. My mom and Carmen came in, each with a casserole dish in hand.

My mom set her dish on the coffee table and sat beside me to give me a hug. "How are you girls doing?"

I gave her a half smile and shrugged. "Better than yesterday. How did you find out about what happened?"

She glanced up at Sadie's mom, Carmen, as she came back out of the kitchen. "Veron came by after he left the shop. Is Sadie still asleep?"

I gave her a quick nod. "I think Binx stayed with her last night. She was pretty freaked out."

Colin stood. "I'll go wake them up."

Carmen nodded. "Thank you, Colin."

My mom slid back farther on the couch. "Veron said Sadie got a good look at that man's eyes. I know it was pretty scary, but I'm glad she noticed. That's the biggest clue we've found since Grams was killed. We've had zero leads to go on for so long."

Sadie, Luca, and Colin came down the hall, and Carmen jumped up to give her daughter a big hug. After a few moments, she let go. "Are you okay?"

Sadie shrugged. "Yeah, better than I was yesterday. Has the GWP found him yet?"

Carmen shook her head. "Your dad and Elijah are at the GWP trying to find a way to weaken his powers while he's in our realm. The GWP can't make a move until they know more about him and his powers. Right now, we wouldn't stand a chance if we tried to take him on. They are looking over Luca's and Colin's memory reports about when they were pulled to that realm."

I jerked my gaze toward at Luca and Colin. "They have your memories?"

Colin nodded. "I was unconscious most of the time we were there, but Luca was awake. They should be able to get info from his memories. It's just a lot of data to go through."

"It will probably take them another forty-eight hours. They hope to have a plan of action by this weekend," Carmen said.

Sadie lifted her brow in confusion. "Won't he go into hiding before then?"

Carmen gave her a quick nod. "It's very possible, but he will show up again at some point. He wants the spell book too badly to just walk away. You two need to get as much training in as you can. Luca and Colin will stay close until you are fully proficient, but you need to learn how to fight back. We aren't sure if this is just one person or a group."

Sadie glanced at Luca then back at Carmen. "We can start training tonight. Neva said she would help out at the shop as much as possible. I need to finish making a few remedies, but that shouldn't take long."

I looked at Colin. "Can we start learning some of the basics here at the house tonight?"

He smiled. "Yeah, we can work on your stances and basic defense moves."

My mom grabbed my hand. "We have to get back to the GWP and see if we can do anything to help. You can bake both breakfast casseroles at three fifty for around forty-five minutes. We will check back in with you this afternoon. The GWP called in Neva this morning, but she will stop by around three or so today."

I stood, and we said our goodbyes, then I headed into the kitchen to put one of the casseroles into the oven and grab us each a drink. When I came back, Sadie was going over her list of remedy requests.

She stared at the paper for a few moments then glanced at Luca. "Do you remember who made this request?"

Luca's gaze shifted to the paper then back up at Colin. "Didn't those three girls request a potion to get someone to do what they wanted?"

I shot Sadie a quick glance then looked back at Luca and Colin. "Wait a minute, the three girls who were flirting with you?"

Colin laughed. "Flirting with us?"

I gave him a blank stare and nodded. "Yes, they were flirting with you. What exactly does a potion like that allow the caster to do?"

Luca studied my face. "It depends on if that specific person has paranormal powers or not. Why?"

When I met Sadie's gaze, she nodded.

I took a sip of my soda and cleared my throat. "This is just a thought, but what are the odds Tobias sent someone to keep an eye on us? I've never seen those three girls in Salem before, so it would make sense. And if the powers between this realm and theirs are different, maybe the potion they requested is something they can't make."

Luca set his drink on the table. "That's very possible. When Colin and I were in that realm, we could hear Raymond opening the rift about five minutes before we were pulled back to this realm. I managed to get my hands free, but Tobias didn't know. As Raymond was finishing the last line of the spell, I jumped up and punched the guy then ran and grabbed the book off the altar across the room."

Eyes widening, I sat up straight on the couch. "Was it a spell book?"

Luca shook his head. "I don't know. It was written in a different language that I can't read. I'm not sure if the GWP looked into it more. I'll call Celeste and ask if they translated it or not."

Sadie raised her brow. "So, what do I do about the potion?"

Colin glanced at Luca then back at Sadie. "Go ahead and mix something we can give them. I'll put a tracking spell on the bottle so we can follow wherever it goes after they pick it up."

Sadie tilted her head and shot Colin a half smile. "I like the way you think. I'll mix the potion's ingredients but not do the spell to activate them."

"You should only do half the amount of one ingredient, in case they can do the spell," I suggested.

"That's a good idea. I'm glad you thought about that," she said.

I smirked and shrugged. "I'll grab the herbs from the apothecary cabinet in the dining room to work on before we start practicing our defensive moves."

Chapter Four

Monday, June 26, 2023

Izzy

I headed into the shop's front room and turned on my desk lamp. It was only eight thirty, and I didn't want to turn on the ceiling lights until we opened. Retrieving the money from the safe, I counted out the starting amount for the day.

Colin brought in my breakfast and put it on my desk then helped me sort the change. He kissed me on the cheek as I closed the cash drawer. "Go eat before you do anything else."

I raised my brow. "Is that a request or an order?"

He paused and gave me a cheeky grin. "It's an order."

"Yes, sir."

His eyes widened. "I like the sound of that."

He tried to keep a straight face but chuckled when I stuck out my tongue at him. He pulled Sadie's chair over to my desk and sat to eat with me. We finished eating and went to the kitchen to toss our trash.

Luca turned to Colin. "Are you ready to do this tracking spell so Sadie can call and let them know it's ready for pick up?"

Colin nodded and sat at the island, where Sadie pulled the potion from her bag and set it on the counter. Luca moved it into the center of the island, and he and Colin slipped their black onyx rings onto their fingers. They pointed their rings toward the bottle and said, "*Indago.*"

Luca pulled out his phone, pushed a couple of buttons, and put it up to his ear. "It's ready. Start the trace. Let me know when you have it, and we will call to let those girls know it's ready." He hung up and stared at the potion bottle.

I tilted my head at Colin. "So, what does that word 'indago' mean?"

He glanced at the bottle then back at me. "It's Latin for 'track' or 'trace.' Once a trace is attached to it, the bottle will glow for about ten seconds, and we will know it's ready."

"Then Sadie can call the girls to pick it up?" I looked at the stove clock. It was 8:54, and we were supposed to open at nine. "Will the tracking spell be active by the time we open?"

Colin gave me a quick nod. "Yeah. It should be done any minute now."

I leaned my elbows onto the counter, and when I went to say something to Colin, the countertop vibrated a bit. The potion glowed a faint purple for about five seconds before it faded.

Luca's phone dinged, and he nodded at Sadie. "You can call the girls. It's ready to go."

Sadie pulled the list of requests from her bag and grabbed her phone, then walked into the front room to call the number. A couple of minutes later, she came back into the kitchen. "They'll be here around nine thirty."

Luca grabbed his phone and typed out a text then looked back up at us. "The GWP will let us know if they think the girls are suspicious or not."

"I hope they won't be able to tell that it's missing anything," I said.

Luca shook his head. "They won't unless they know exactly what goes in it and how to make it. But almost every potion you can make has multiple recipes. People use different ingredients in their own recipes, so they shouldn't notice."

"That's very true." I walked into the front room and turned on the lights, unlocking the door before going back toward the kitchen with Colin. "Can we work on some charging spells while we wait?"

He winked. "I'll be right there. I hope you're ready."

I spun to face Sadie.

She shrugged and smiled. "You asked for it, I guess."

Taking a deep breath, I headed to my desk. Colin was at the jewelry case containing the pocket stones, slid the cabinet closed and came to sit in Sadie's chair at my desk. He opened his hand, revealing an obsidian stone.

I took the stone and gave him a puzzled glance. "What am I charging this with?"

He stared blankly for a moment, then his eyes widened. "Let's do one for protection and defense. Do you have your journal?"

I nodded and grabbed my bag from under the desk, pulling out my journal with the binding spell in it that had the number two on the spine. Pops gave it to me in the last package that Izzy and I had received from him. I laid it on the desk and looked at Colin. "Will I need any other spells that I've done?"

He gave a quick nod. "Yes, I want to see how you go about doing the intentions for this one. You can look at previous spells if you need to."

I pulled out my journal with the number one on the spine and laid it on my desk, opening it to the spells that Pops had us work on. "So, you want me to write how to do a charging spell for protection and defense?"

"Yep. I'll be right here if you need help. You can write it just like Raymond wrote his."

Nodding, I opened my new journal to the page after the notes I had written on the binding spell. I referred back to my first journal and started writing.

Obsidian stone: _provides protection and defense_

Hold the stone in your dominant hand and focus on the intentions you want the stone to have. For an absorbing charge, you will want your intention to be as follows:

"My intention for this obsidian stone is to provide protection to me by allowing me to block any and all forms of danger that are aimed toward me."

I gave Colin a nervous smile as he leaned back in his chair.

"Will this work?" I slid the journal toward him, and he sat up to see it better.

As he read, his eyes widened, and he tilted his head a bit then glanced at me. "This is really good. Since you wrote these intentions yourself, you get to decide how to activate it."

I looked at the obsidian stone around my neck that I had made to absorb energy blasts. "It would be nice to have it active at all times, kinda like the protection bag Sadie made."

He gave a quick nod and gestured toward the journal page. "Okay, you need to write that down with the instructions. You also need to write the instructions on how to make it into a talisman."

I started writing again.

Then you want to imagine your intention flowing into the stone and absorbing it like a sponge.

Your stone is always active and would be best used as a necklace to avoid dropping it and it being out of reach.

*If you are charging the stone for someone else as a talisman, when setting the intentions, you would say their name with he or she as needed.

I reread what I had written, and the words on the page started to glow a bright red for about two seconds, then faded into a dark magenta before going back to the black ink. I gave Colin a confused glance. "What was that?"

He smiled broadly and placed his hand over mine. "That, Miss Isadora Monroe, is your very first spell."

I looked down at the words again. "But why does it glow like that?"

The corners of his mouth twitched. "Because no one else has ever written a charging spell with those exact words. So, once the complete spell is written for the first time, it glows your paranormal color."

I tried not to focus too much on biting his lip like he was. "I think you guys should ask the girls out to dinner to see if they mention anything about the spell book."

Sadie and Luca entered the front room, and Colin got up to let Sadie have her chair.

Luca tapped him on the shoulder before looking at me. "What do you want us to do?"

Colin's brow rose. "She said we should take those girls out to dinner to see if they mention anything about the spell book."

Luca shrugged. "I guess we could do that. At least see if they know about it."

Colin scratched the side of his face. "How do you know they'll want to go out with us?"

I smiled and nudged Colin. "I saw the way they looked at you when they came in Saturday. The two younger blondes wouldn't stop flirting."

Luca elbowed Colin. "I guess our girls didn't believe us when we told them we only had eyes for them."

I rolled my eyes. "You may only have eyes for us, but they certainly had their eyes on you two."

Colin let out a growl. "Fine. We'll take them out."

Sadie smiled at them then leaned in to see what I was working on.

I slid my journal in front of her. "When I finished writing this charging spell, the words glowed a bright magenta for a few seconds."

As Sadie leaned forward to read the spell, the bells above the front door jingled. She glanced up and gasped.

Chapter Five
Monday, June 26, 2023

Sadie

For a split second, I thought Tobias was at the window again as I looked at the two blondes walking to the register.

"Hi. Are you here to pick up your potion?" I asked.

The taller girl nodded as she placed her wallet on the upper ledge of the counter. "I'm Maggie, and this is Beth." She glanced toward the kitchen. "Are your helpers not here today?"

I gave her a puzzled look. "Helpers?"

She nodded. "Yes, those two cuties who took my order Friday."

I lifted my head a bit. "Oh yes. They're in the kitchen." I reached down and grabbed the potion from beside the register and placed it in a small paper bag. "Your order total is thirty-six dollars and fifty cents."

She threw two twenty-dollar bills onto the counter just as the guys came into the front room.

Colin came up to the register beside me and leaned against the counter. "Well, hello again, ladies. I'm glad you stopped back by.

My buddy Luca and I wanted to see if you would grab a bite to eat with us after we close tonight."

Beth leaned forward, placing her hand on Colin's. "We would be thrilled to join you. We'll meet you out front at six."

She grabbed the bag, and they turned toward the exit. As they walked out, she winked at Colin before the door closed behind her.

Izzy shrugged. "Now I'm wondering if they just placed the order so they could see you two again."

I nodded and turned to find Luca and Colin watching us.

Luca glanced at the cash on the ledge. "She's an odd one. I guess we will find out soon if she's involved."

"Yes, they are odd. They have to be the ones Celeste said were supposed to be making contact at the grand reopening. They were the only ones who didn't seem like they intentionally came in to buy something."

Luca pulled out his phone and dialed a number. "She has the bottle. Can you see it moving?" He paused. "Okay, good. Keep me updated as often as you can." He hung up and slid his phone back into his pocket. "They can see it moving. He said the girls are still on Main Street right now."

I gave Luca another quick nod then heard the kitchen door open and turned to see Neva walking in with a scruffy man in his late fifties.

I smiled and waved. "Hey, Neva."

She walked over to lay her purse on the island and entered the front room with us, putting her hand on the man's arm as she smiled. "This is Cyrus. He works in security for the GWP and is an unbound familiar."I stood and held out my hand. "It's nice to meet you, Cyrus."

He shook my hand. "Nice to meet you as well. Please excuse my appearance. I'm not normally quite this poorly dressed or unprofessional."

Neva smiled and leaned into him. "He's undercover for the GWP. They hope that if Cyrus stays near us and unbound, Tobias will try calling upon him to steal the spell book."

My eyes widened, and I glanced at Izzy, who tilted her head at Cyrus.

"And you're okay with that?" she asked.

Cyrus gave her a half smile and nodded. "Yes, I've been with the GWP's security team for one hundred ten years now. If I'm in trouble, I can turn into my familiar form to defend myself."

I shot Neva a puzzled expression before returning to Cyrus. "How would you take them out? What type of cat are you in familiar form, a lion?"

Cyrus chuckled. "Oh god, no. I'm not a cat. I'm a cane corso. Familiars can be different types of animals."

Izzy's eyebrows furrowed. "Cane corso, that's a dog, right?"

Cyrus nodded. "Yes. In my familiar form, I am two hundred pounds of solid muscle and razor-sharp teeth, and despite my size, I'm very quick."

Izzy raised her brow. "That's pretty impressive. So, the GWP thinks that Tobias will try contacting you. Why?"

Cyrus leaned against the side of Izzy's desk. "The work I do for the GWP is sometimes frowned upon. I've done a lot of bad things over the years, but everything was done with good intentions."

Izzy raised her brows. "I'm guessing you've killed people."

Cyrus looked down and gave a quick nod. "Only people on the evil side. Killing them still wasn't easy or something I'm proud of, but it had to be done to save someone or prevent something bad from happening."

I cut in before Izzy could question Cyrus more. "Well, I'm glad you're willing to help."

He smiled. "It's my pleasure."

I turned to Luca, who was typing on his phone.

"Tyson said the girls went into one of the apartments over the Bean & Bake," he said. "I wonder if Donald and Mel know who they are. I thought the two apartments were occupied by elderly couples."

Colin nodded. "I thought so too. Maybe their grandparents live there."

Luca tilted his head. "That's possible, I guess. But it's still strange. The GWP will keep an eye on them, and I'm sure they will contact Donald and Mel about it."

Neva gave a heavy sigh. "They'll have to ask Donald. Mel is in the medical ward with a fairly bad concussion. She was taking the trash out two nights ago at the coffee shop, and Donald found her lying in the middle of the alley beside the dumpster. She doesn't remember what happened aside from seeing a bright light then waking up on the way to the hospital."

Izzy gasped and walked over to give Neva a hug. "Will she be okay? Why didn't we hear about this sooner?"

Neva nodded. "She didn't want anyone to know until they figured out what happened. The doctor said she will be fine, but she may not get her memories back. I was terrified when I found out. I'm not ready to lose my best friend."

"Poor Mel. I know how scary not remembering things can be after something like that. I still don't have a clear recollection of that warlock knocking me out," Izzy said.

I put my hand on Luca's arm and leaned closer to him. "I'm going to go call the other people who made requests to let them know they can pick up their orders."

He gave me a quick nod, and I went into the kitchen to call the people on the list. Izzy came in a few seconds later and sat beside me at the island. I wrote what time each customer would be in to pick up their orders. Once I made the calls, I headed back to my desk and started a list of items that I needed to get from Barnaby's while the guys chatted with Cyrus.

I tried to focus on my list, but I couldn't help but hear Cyrus's plan. It seemed like a suicide mission, and I hoped Tobias wouldn't take his life or anyone else's. He already had enough blood on his hands.

"Cyrus is the best of the best. Don't you worry about him. He can take care of himself," Luca said telepathically, causing me to jump.

"How do you do that? You weren't supposed to hear that," I replied.

"You weren't exactly thinking quietly on that one," he said.

I turned to glance into the kitchen, where he stood beside Colin, and my face flushed. He caught my gaze, and his magnetism sent shivers down my spine, warming my core. I would never get tired of that feeling. And just as I thought it, he winked at me as if he had heard my thoughts again then looked away, breaking our connection. I sighed and went back to my list for Barnaby's.

Chapter Six

Monday, June 26, 2023

Colin

After Neva and Cyrus settled in to watch the shop, Izzy and Sadie got ready for training and went to the kitchen door with their bags to wait for me and Luca.

Luca stopped at the door that led up to the second floor. "Where are you two going? We have to train."

Sadie furrowed her brows in confusion. "I thought we were training at the GWP."

Luca shook his head. "Not today we aren't. You coming?"

She stared at him for a moment before hanging her bag on the back of the bar-stool, then she gestured toward the door and bowed her head. "After you."

Luca opened the door to climb the stairs, and Izzy and Sadie followed.

"How are we supposed to train upstairs?" Sadie asked.

Luca turned to me as he reached the second-floor door, grinning sheepishly as he pushed it open. "See for yourselves, ladies."

Izzy and Sadie stepped into the room and gasped.

Izzy turned toward me. "When did you guys have time to do this?"

The last time the girls had come up to the second floor was when we were putting everything on the shelves after their dads finished the repairs. There had been a few boxes, two-by-fours, and dust. Now the area was clean, with mats covering the center of the room. The area over the kitchen was lined with shelves and a large table in the center where Izzy could paint.

Luca smiled. "It wasn't us."

Sadie jerked her head toward Izzy then back to Luca. "If it wasn't you two, who did it?" she asked.

I wrapped my arm around Izzy's shoulders. "Your parents." I stared at them for another moment. "Now, any more questions, or can we get to training?"

The girls nodded and stepped up to the edge of the mat, slipping off their shoes. Luca and I walked up behind them and handed each of them a bag.

"What are these?" Sadie peeked into the bag.

Luca gave a little smile. "Workout clothes. Go get changed."

She shook her head. "You two were way too prepared for this, but thank you." She looked at Izzy. "You can go first."

Izzy gave her a quick nod and headed to the bathroom. Sadie started pulling the clothes from the bag and taking off the tags on a light-purple sports bra with splashes of darker purple all over, a purple tank top, and workout shorts, and she smiled at Luca.

"It's kind of creepy that you know so much about our likes and dislikes."

Izzy came out of the bathroom, and she was dressed in an outfit like Sadie's, but it was shades of red and pink instead of purple. She looked at me. "I agree with Sadie. But I love it. Thank you."

Sadie gave Luca a kiss on the cheek. "Thank you." Turning, she headed to the bathroom to change and came back out a couple of minutes later to stand beside Izzy on the mats.

Luca and I went to the bathroom next to change into our shorts then joined the girls a minute later on the mat.

I could tell they were sore from training the night before. "Let's do some warm-up stretches before we start today."

They nodded and got into position.

"Let's start with arm circles," I said.

Izzy giggled and whispered to Sadie, who nodded and smiled.

I raised my brow and cleared my throat. "Is there anything you would like to share with the class?"

Izzy's face went blank, and I chuckled. "Okay, now cross your right arm over your chest and pull it tight with your left arm. Hold this for fifteen seconds." I winked at Izzy, and she seemed to relax a bit. "Now switch arms and hold." I found myself struggling to not stare at Izzy. Reds and pinks looked so good on her, and they brought out the natural glow about her. It was definitely her signature color. She looked beautiful.

After ten minutes of stretches, we were warmed up. I pointed to the front corner of the room. "Go grab a bottle of water from the fridge, then we'll start training."

The girls opened the fridge, and Sadie turned to shake her head at me and Luca before grabbing two bottles of water. They returned to the mat, Sadie handing Luca a bottle while Izzy gave me one.

"What was that look for?" I asked Sadie.

She shook her head again. "Our parents somehow did all of this without us knowing. That fridge wasn't here the last time we came up here."

Luca nodded. "Yeah, they did. They also ordered some mirrors for the wall. Mr. Plum should be here Wednesday to install them."

Sadie's eyebrows rose. "Why didn't they tell us about all of this?"

"I'm not sure," Luca said. "They mentioned it to us the night we dropped off your last package from Raymond, and they texted us last night to tell us it was ready aside from the mirrors. They wanted you to feel comfortable training."

Sadie shrugged. "Okay, I guess we need to get used to them keeping secrets. Can we just get started on training?"

Luca and I nodded and stood before them.

I took a sip of water and set it aside. "You can defend yourselves using a bunch of different punches and kicks, but we'll start with three basic ones—the front kick, the side kick, and the back kick. Kicks are mainly used for long range. If an enemy is coming toward you, kick. It might not stop him, but it should slow him down."

I nodded at Luca, gesturing for him to take over. He was always better at teaching punches.

"Punches are your close-range defense. We will start with three basic ones for those as well. They are the straight punch, the hook punch, and the uppercut. We'll begin with punches then incorporate the kicks slowly."

After learning the drills and practicing for a few minutes, Izzy stopped to grab a drink of water. When she walked back over, she stood a few feet away. "Why are you moving so slow? Are you going easy on me again?"

How could she think I'm going easy on her? I am having to fight back the urge to pull her close to me and kiss her crazy every time our bodies touch, but I don't think I'm taking it easy. I tried to catch her off guard by sneaking a punch toward her side. She blocked it and punched back. I blocked it and caught a glimpse of fire in her that I hadn't seen before. As I threw a couple more blows and a kick toward her, she fought back, defending herself perfectly.

I kept it up for another thirty seconds before I tried to stop so she could take a break. But Izzy continued throwing punches and kicks. Ducking around, I grabbed her from behind to calm her down. Pinning her arms tight against her body, I lifted her feet off the ground. She stilled as if to stop, and I loosened my grip a bit when I felt her take a deep breath. A second later, as she released that breath, we flew backward, and I landed on my back on the mat six feet from where we stood. She lay on top of me, breathing heavily.

Sadie gasped and ran over to us, helping Izzy up as I slowly got to my feet.

"Oh my god! Colin, are you okay? What happened?" Izzy asked, her face riddled with confusion.

Sadie jerked her gaze toward me in shock then glanced back at Izzy. "You don't know?"

She looked down and rubbed the side of her head. "The last thing I remember was throwing punches with him."

Luca tapped me on the back. "Are you okay?"

"Yes. I think I just unlocked another one of Izzy's elemental powers Raymond told us she might have."

Sadie raised her brow. "What are you talking about?"

I grabbed my water and took a drink. "Raymond told us that he thought you two had the ability to wield all the elements to your will. I didn't believe it at first because I've never met anyone who could wield all five. It's a very rare power."

Sadie stared at me in confusion. "I didn't even see her do anything. I just heard you two hit the mat. How did she wield an element?"

I took another drink of my water. "When we were throwing punches, I slowed down so she could take a break, but she kept going. It was like she was in a daze. I'm not sure why, but then, when I grabbed her from behind and lifted her off the ground, she took a deep breath. I thought she was coming out of her daze, but when she released that breath, it threw us backward. It was like we were pushed really hard."

Luca tilted his head and scrunched his face. "I wonder if the daze could have been her ESP."

"What is that?" Sadie asked Luca.

"Extrasensory perception. You both can block every kick and punch we throw at you. It's like you know it's coming even before we start the movement. We have worked with grown men who couldn't block that well, even after working with them for weeks—and they all had prior training of some kind."

I smiled at the girls. "Don't worry. This is great news. You both will still need to train, but when it comes to defending yourselves, you can already tell what type of punch or kick is coming at you. That is the hard part most people take time to learn."

Izzy put her head on my arm. "I feel awful about throwing you back like that, though."

I chuckled and wrapped my arms around her. "Don't feel bad. I'm actually impressed. It will take more than that to hurt me." I kissed the top of her head and hugged her a little tighter.

Luca finished his bottle of water and tossed it in the trash. "We should get changed and head back downstairs. You're already ahead with training. When we get back to the house this afternoon, we can read more about wielding the elements in the books Raymond gave you."

Luca and I changed back into our jeans while the girls got dressed in the bathroom. We all went downstairs together. Sadie seemed excited about finding out they were ahead with training and that they had extrasensory perception. Izzy seemed to be in deep thought about how she had used her air power without knowing. It would be a while before she could fully wield her powers, but she was catching on quickly. I wrapped my arm around her when we reached the bottom step and leaned down to kiss the side of her head.

"Don't worry about how you did that. Just be proud of yourself that you did," I whispered.

Chapter Seven

Monday, June 26, 2023

Luca

As I walked to the front of the shop to lock the doors, I saw Maggie and Beth sitting on the bench in the middle of Main Street next to the fountain. I flipped off the lights and slid the sign to *closed* before going to help clean up.

I released a heavy sigh. "Are you two sure we should be going out with those girls?"

Sadie giggled. "Well, yeah. How else will we know if they're working for the demon?"

"We could just wait until they make a move. That's how we used to do things. We never just went out on a date with someone to find out if they were evil," I said as she wiped down the island.

Colin nudged me. "It's not a date per say. It's just a meal with some Roots & Remedies customers."

I let out another long breath. "I guess that's a good way to look at it. It takes the pressure off." I looked at Colin. "Are you almost ready? They're already out there."

Colin nodded and leaned down to kiss Izzy on the head. "I'll see you in a couple of hours, sunshine. Don't work too hard while I'm gone."

"I won't." She laid her head on his chest and hugged him.

I shook my head in disbelief. I couldn't believe how soft Colin was these days. It was like he had turned into a powder puff with Izzy by his side.

As I turned to Sadie, someone knocked at the front door. "Ugh. I guess we better go before they get too impatient." I gave her a quick smirk and leaned in to kiss her cheek, then paused and stared at Sadie for a moment as I realized I was getting just as soft as Colin.

"Have fun, you two, and please be careful," she said and kissed my cheek.

I gave her a quick wink, and Colin and I headed toward the front door. Sadie locked it behind us.

Maggie came up and put her hand on my chest. "Well hello, handsome. Where would you like to go to eat?"

Colin stopped in front of Beth and glanced down Main Street toward the Mexican restaurant there. "Do you two like Mexican food?"

Their eyes went wide, and they hooked their arms with ours.

"Love it!" they said in unison as we started walking down Main Street.

Thoughts flooded my head about how this pretend date would go. *How will I react if Maggie tries to kiss me? My heart is with Sadie, and I would never have feelings for someone like either one of these two girls. Why did I agree to this?*

The hostess sat us at the back corner booth, gave us our menus, and took our drink orders.

Maggie leaned a little closer to me and whispered, "I'm gonna run to the ladies' room really quick. Don't you try sneaking off."

I gave her a quick smile and a slight nod. The comment caught me a little off guard. *Why would she think I'd try to sneak off?*

About two minutes later, Maggie approached our table with our tray of drinks. I shot Colin a quick glance before looking back at Maggie. "Why are you bringing our drinks?"

A toothy grin formed on her face, but she didn't answer. I took my drink from her, and she handed Colin and Beth theirs, leaving the tray at the edge of the table before sliding in beside me.

I grabbed a straw from the pile in the center of the table as I telepathically voiced my thoughts to Colin. "*Drink it slowly. If she put something in it, we'll know pretty quickly, but I don't want to raise their suspicion.*"

Colin's eyes met mine for a split second. "*I have a bad feeling about this.*"

We tried making small talk as we waited for our food. The longer we sat there, the flirtier the girls got.

Colin was starting to fidget. "*I think they might have put a love potion in our drinks. Should we kinda flirt back so they think it's working?*"

"*Yeah, I don't wanna blow our chances of finding out if they're involved with Tobias.*"

He took a deep breath and turned toward Beth a little more. "So, Beth, what activities do you like to do?"

She gave him a cheeky grin. "Well, I am really into reading these days. I discovered some interesting books at the library recently."

Colin took a sip of his drink. "Oh yeah? What were they about?"

She placed her hand over his. "They're about the history of the Salem witches who lived here back in the 1600s. It's very interesting. But unfortunately, the book I wanted to read the most wasn't in there."

I raised my brows, pretending to be interested. "We've lived here all our lives. What book is it? Maybe we can help you find it."

She gave a quick shrug. "I don't think it has an official title. It's more of a journal or diary-type book. From what I read, a witch named Hazel Craig wrote a bunch of spells to help people with things like their illnesses or their problems in life. My mom has been sick for a long time, and the doctors don't know what's wrong. I hoped that book would have something in it I could try. Our uncle is the one who told us about it. He said that he would help us make the remedy if we could find the book."

I wasn't completely sure what it was about the way she said it, but she actually seemed sincere—until she mentioned her uncle. Maybe Tobias had tricked them into thinking he would help them, or maybe this was how they'd planned to get it from the start, so we didn't offer to help them.

I met Colin's gaze and smiled. "I think I know that exact book and its location. I just need an hour or so to get it. I can go right after we eat, then I can meet you at the corner of Chester Street and Bennington Avenue."

Beth's expression turned giddy, and she started quietly clapping and bouncing in her seat. She reached over and put her hand on top of mine. "Oh my gosh. You two are so sweet to do that for me. Thank you so much. We can meet you there."

The server walked up and passed out our meals. We continued making small talk and flirting as we ate. Once we finished, we walked the girls back to the Bean & Bake, and they disappeared into the alley with the door that led to the apartments. Colin and I headed back to the house, where Sadie and Izzy were waiting for us.

Chapter Eight
Monday, June 26, 2023

Sadie

Since the guys were out on their pretend date with the two girls, Izzy and I decided to work on the code Pops left us. So far, we had tried all the Goosebumps books, but none of their page numbers went high enough. The Nancy Drew books had a few that did, but none of the numbers lined up to anything that made sense. Even when we tried to decipher the code with our codex from Pops.

We had just started going through the cookbooks when the guys came back. The expression on their faces confirmed our suspicions.

Luca plopped down beside me on the love seat in Pops's office and sighed heavily. "You were right about them. They are definitely after Hazel Craig's spell book."

I laid the cookbook on the end table. "What did they say?"

Colin leaned against the desk beside Izzy. "Beth wants to check the spell book for any spells that will help her mother, who is supposedly sick and the doctors don't know what is wrong with her."

"Did she say anything about anyone else wanting it?" Izzy sipped her drink.

"No, but she did say her uncle would help her with the remedy. I've gotta call Celeste and run a plan by her." Luca pulled his phone from his pocket. Moments later, he had filled her in on the dinner and what the girls had said about wanting the spell book, then he looked at me. "Do you know if Raymond had any old material that we could wrap around a big book?"

I nodded, and Izzy slid the box out from under the desk where she sat. Luca was quiet again then told Celeste where he was supposed to meet the girls with the book. After another minute, he hung up and said the plan was in motion.

"What if she's telling the truth about her mother being sick and somehow Tobias tricked them?" The thought filled me with concern.

Luca took my hand. "Once we get them in custody, they will be questioned and the information will be verified. The GWP will help her mom in any way possible if they find out she is indeed sick."

"I couldn't imagine using my parents in a scenario like that and it not being true." Chills rolled up my arms.

Luca pulled me close to him. "Evil knows no bounds."

Colin

Luca and I left the house with the fake spell book wrapped in an old piece of cloth and headed to the corner of Bennington Avenue and Chester Street. We were a few minutes early, so we sat on the bench against the old empty building on the corner.

Maggie and Beth arrived about five minutes later. Maggie reached out and tried to touch the cloth covering the book. The look in her eyes was more sinister than when Beth had been talking about it at the restaurant.

I leaned away, moving the book from her reach, and turned my attention to Beth. "I thought you were the one who wanted to see the book, Beth."

Maggie huffed. "Well, duh. I want my mom to be better too."

My brows shot up. "Oh, you didn't mention anything about you two being sisters. That makes more sense."

Maggie reached for the book again, and once she had it in her hands, she started laughing. "I can't believe how easy it was to get from you two." She waved her hand and mumbled something in another language.

She and Beth turned to run off and walked right into the arms of the two security guards assigned to help us. James, the guard who had Maggie, took the book from her and offered it to me. When I attempted to step forward to accept it, my feet were locked in place, and so were Luca's.

James gripped her arm tighter, pulling her up. "Release that spell, right now."

Maggie grunted but lifted her hand and said something else in the language I didn't recognize.

I stepped forward and took the book from James.

Maggie smiled. "This isn't over, ya know. If we fail to get the spell book, Tobias will be coming next. And he won't be as nice or as pretty as we are." She stood straight and pushed out her chest.

I rolled my eyes and looked over at James. "Take them to Paxton. They won't be so flirty after he's done with them."

Chapter Nine
Tuesday, June 27, 2023

Izzy

We pulled up to the shop at half past eight. We still had half an hour before we opened for the day, so we sat at the island for a quick bite to eat.

Luca ran his fingers through his hair while staring down at his phone. "Celeste said we can train in the GWP arena as much as we want. She will also have one of the senior trainers send us some pointers on ways to hone you on your elemental powers."

I grabbed bowls out of the cabinet then set them on the island. "So, what's the plan for training? Do we train here for the rest of the week and then go out to the arena on Sunday?" I grabbed the milk from the fridge before sitting down at the corner of the island beside Colin.

Sadie looked at Luca. "That sounds good to me. I just need to spend a little time in the backyard. The next bunch of herbs and flowers are almost ready for cutting."

"Maybe Neva can watch the shop Friday morning, and I can help you." I grabbed spoons from the drawer and passed them out.

Sadie nodded as she poured the milk over her cereal. "I'll ask her when she gets here if she's available. I don't know what the GWP has her doing with Cyrus, but I'm guessing that takes priority right now."

"As far as I know, Cyrus is just following her around. They're supposed to be acting like a couple—holding hands and flirting while they're in public. The GWP wants Tobias and his spies to see them together for a little while, and they hope he tries to call on Cyrus while he's not with Neva." Colin took a big bite of his cereal. "Is that what you understood from Celeste's call, Luca?"

Luca nodded and swallowed. "Yeah, that's the way I took it."

Sadie dropped her spoon onto the counter to rub her arms. "Every time I think of his eyes, it sends chills all over my body."

Luca pulled her into his arms. "The faster we get this demon, the better."

I nodded and took a bite of my cereal, then moved the marshmallows around my bowl before I peeked up at Sadie. I couldn't begin to imagine what she must have felt. I wished I could have seen him too. I was the only one who hadn't actually seen the black-eyed creep in person.

Colin and Luca had been held hostage by him, and Sadie had seen him twice. I didn't honestly know if I would recognize him with just the description they'd given. A cold chill shot down my back, and I sat up straighter, trying to wipe the image of a random pair of black eyes staring at me from my mind.

Taking the last bite of my cereal, I got up to dump the milk in the sink and set the bowl on the counter before turning to Colin. "I just hope Cyrus is as strong as he said he is. I don't want him to get hurt."

"Cyrus is very strong. I've never seen him in action, but I've heard stories." Colin took his last bite of cereal and brought his bowl to the sink. "Are you ready to work on your next spell?"

I gave him a quick nod and turned to Sadie. "I'll be out front if you need me."

Colin grabbed my hand and pulled me toward my desk before she could answer.

"Hey, what's the big hurry?"

He let go of my hand and walked around to the jewelry case, slid the door open, and bent to look inside. "This next spell is pretty neat."

A weird tingle awakened in my lower stomach, and my heart fluttered. Colin wore his normal tight white tank top and baggy black jeans, but something about the way he leaned into the jewelry case caught me off guard. He quickly straightened and slid the case closed then held a moonstone between his two fingers for me to see.

"Wha—" I cleared my throat and gave my head a slight shake. "Um. What is that for?" I took a deep breath and closed my eyes to regain my senses while I waited for his reply.

When I opened my eyes again, he stood right in front of me. I gasped and jumped back.

He grabbed my arm to steady me. "Izzy, are you okay?"

"Yes, I just need a drink of water. I think I should have eaten something with less sugar this morning." I gave Colin a half smile, hoping he hadn't seen me staring at him. I didn't know why I was so flustered. It wasn't the first time I'd watched him bend over like that.

He gave me a weird look and guided me to my chair. As he walked into the kitchen, I tried to calm my racing heart. I could hear the fridge door open then close. He came back into the front room and set a water bottle on my desk, then pulled Sadie's chair over to sit beside me. Grabbing my bag from the back of my chair, I pulled out my journals and got everything situated on my desk. I could feel Colin's gaze on me and slowly turned to find his eyebrows raised.

"What?" I asked.

He glanced at the bottle of water then back to me. "I thought you needed a drink of water."

The back of my neck warmed, and my cheeks flushed. I grabbed the bottle of water and took a gulp, trying to ignore the heat coming from my neck and cheeks. "Okay, so, what are we charging the moonstone with?" I turned my head toward him but avoided eye contact. I could still feel his gaze on me.

He laid the moonstone on top of my journals. "You need this stone to guide you to your destination and have it light your way in the process. How do you charge it?"

"Um. I would—" I turned to him, and he shook his head. "What's wrong?"

He gave me a half smile and tucked my hair behind my ear. "I don't want you to tell me. I want you to write the spell."

My cheeks flushed more as I dropped my gaze from Colin to my journals. Grabbing my pen and the moonstone, I opened my journal to the next empty page and started to write. I wrote the name of the stone and what it would be used for before another red-hot wave came over me. I dropped my pen and slumped back in my chair.

Colin leaned toward me and put his hand on my forehead. "Sadie, I need you in here!" he yelled.

Then everything went black.

Chapter Ten
Tuesday, June 27, 2023

Sadie

I quickly walked into the front room and saw Colin pressing his palm to Izzy's forehead. "Oh my god. Is she okay?" I squatted beside the chair, and he moved around to the other side.

Colin shrugged. "She started acting off a couple of minutes ago, and I thought she was just flustered. She was staring at me when I bent to look in the jewelry case. I didn't call her out on it because I know how easily she gets embarrassed." He ran his fingers through his hair. "I don't know if it's a lingering effect from the concussion Warrick gave her in the cemetery or if this is another power taking hold. I've never seen one have this effect on someone."

I watched as Izzy's eyes moved back and forth behind her closed eyelids. It was like she was dreaming. "Did she pass out, or did she fall asleep?"

"She was writing in her journal then dropped her pen onto the desk and leaned back. Her face and the back of her neck were really red." Colin jumped up to grab a washcloth from the bathroom linen closet and got it wet. He wiped the back of her neck and her cheeks and put the cool rag on her forehead.

"Should we lay her down on the floor so she doesn't fall out of the chair?"

"Yes, that's a good idea." Colin moved her chair so she could be placed where she wouldn't be seen from the front door.

Then Luca and Colin gently lowered her from the chair to the floor. I grabbed her bag from the back of her chair and placed it under her head. Her eyes still fluttered back and forth behind her eyelids.

I looked up at Luca. "Can you grab my phone from the kitchen please?"

He gave me a quick nod, and a moment later, he was handing me my phone. I unlocked it, pulled up Sylvia's number, and hit the green button.

It rang a few times before she answered. "Hey, Sadie, is everything okay?"

"I don't know. Izzy and Colin were in the front room, and she was writing in her journal and working on a new spell, and Colin said she got really red and passed out. Her breathing and pulse seem okay, but her eyes are going back and forth behind her eyelids like she's dreaming. I don't know what to do." I put my hand on Izzy's cheek.

"Your mom and I will be there in a few minutes. Try to keep her still, and put something under her head." She hung up before I could say anything else.

"Our moms will be here in a couple minutes," I said.

Colin sat on the floor beside Izzy, and Luca took a seat beside me as he kissed me on the cheek.

"Will she be okay?"

Luca shrugged. "I'm not sure. I have no clue what's going on. She was fine fifteen minutes ago."

Colin grabbed Izzy's hand and moved a strand of hair out of her face. "It's like she's dreaming, but there's no way she fell asleep that fast. It was maybe five seconds from the time she dropped her pen and leaned back. She seemed a little dizzy right before."

With a gasp, Izzy jerked her hands out of ours and bolted upright. Her face was filled with terror as she looked around. A few seconds later, she wrapped her arms around Colin and started crying. He held her tight and peered up at me and Luca. His brows furrowed in confusion as she slowly released him.

I softly placed my hand on her shoulder, careful not to startle her, and she turned to face me.

"Tobias is a monster. I had no clue why he seemed so scary to you when you saw him at the window, but now, I know."

"Izzy, what are you talking about?" I frowned as she wiped the tears from her eyes.

"I'm not sure exactly what happened, but one moment, I was writing in my journal, and then I was like a ghost in a room with Tobias and another man. He was talking about the spell book and what he wanted to do with it. He said it contains a spell that he can use to bring all his people to our realm. He wants to kill everyone here and take over our world. Something is happening in his—something there is dying." She rubbed her hand over her face and peered up at Luca. "We need to warn Cyrus. Tobias has his eye on him. He thinks he can tempt Cyrus over to his side. He wants Cyrus to help him get the spell book."

Luca pulled his phone out of his pocket. "Did he say anything about you and Sadie?"

"Yes, he said we aren't a threat since we don't have magical powers, like our parents." She shrugged at me. "I guess that spell Pops put on us is working."

Colin flicked his hair out of his face. "Did he say anything about when he plans to attack or anything?"

"He intends to make contact with Cyrus as soon as Cyrus leaves Neva's side. The blondes are working with Tobias. They aren't staying in the apartments over the Bean & Bake. The rift they are using to come to our realm is in the alley beside it."

Luca pushed a couple of buttons on his phone and glanced at Colin. "I'm calling this in." He put the phone to his ear, and after a few moments, he started filling in the person on the other end as he exited to walk toward the greenhouse.

The kitchen door flew open, and we all turned as my mom and Sylvia came rushing into the kitchen. Izzy stood and went into the kitchen with them.

Holding her at an arm's length, Sylvia looked her over before wrapping her arms around her daughter. "I'm so sorry, Izzy. I hoped you wouldn't get this power."

Izzy pulled away from her mom. "Wait, another power?"

Sylvia gestured for us to sit at the island, and Colin went out to the greenhouse to check on Luca.

She leaned against the island and gave a big sigh. "You have the power of second sight, also known as blinking."

"Well, that explains why I could see Tobias, but he didn't seem to know I was watching." She tilted her head and rubbed her eyes.

Sylvia's brows furrowed. "Wait! Is he here in our realm?"

Izzy shook her head.

"So, you can see into other realms?"

Izzy looked down at her hands then up at her mom. "Yeah, I guess so. What does that mean?"

Sylvia leaned in to wrap her arms around Izzy again. "It means you are a lot stronger than we could have imagined." She turned to me. "Just a heads-up—this power normally runs in families. Pops had it, so you probably will get it too."

I rolled my eyes at my mom. "That's just great."

Izzy gave my mom and Sylvia the rundown of what Tobias had said and what his plan was.

Luca came back in from the greenhouse. "Celeste is setting up some extra surveillance around the shop and house. Colin is on the phone now with Cyrus, filling him in on what happened."

Colin came back inside just as Luca finished talking. He slid his phone back into his pocket and closed the door. "Cyrus will go home by way of the alley when they get back from Barnaby's while Neva stays here with us. Cyrus hopes Tobias will try making contact today so we can get more information on the situation."

Luca gave him a quick nod. "Sounds good."

My mom glanced at Luca and Colin and then back at us. "The guys will fill you in on this new power of yours. They can teach you to control it. Don't leave their side. Get in as much training as possible over the next couple of weeks. We will need you ready to go sooner than later." She kissed my cheek and gave me a quick hug. "We have to get back to the GWP to figure out our next steps."

Izzy stood to give her mom a quick hug, and my mom and Sylvia headed out the door. I glanced at the clock on the wall, and it was nine twenty. I headed up front to open the door and turn on the lights.

James, our security guard, sat on the bench across the street in front of Plum's Hardware. He had his hat pulled low and wore dark sunglasses as he held his newspaper in front of him, but I doubted he was actually reading it.

I turned to walk back toward the kitchen as Izzy sat down at her desk.

"Are you okay?" I asked.

She nodded and scratched the top of her head. "Physically? Yes. Mentally? No, not by a long shot. That was worse than that dream I had about him. When I first realized where I was, Tobias stood about three feet away from me. I tried to drop to the floor, and that's when I realized my body wasn't attached to me. I didn't know who he was until he started talking about the spell book and coming to our realm. He looked eviler than in my dreams. The minion he was talking to said something was going to take longer than planned, and that's when Tobias's eyes went black. I jerked back when he looked toward where I was standing. I thought for sure he could see me."

I sat for a moment, trying to figure out what to say to her then leaned in to give her a hug. "I'm so sorry you had to go through that. But hopefully, with this new information, we can take him out when he tries to attack."

She wiped the tear that snuck down her cheek. "Yeah, I hope so. I hope he suffers for what he did to Pops and Grams too."

My eyes went wide at her bluntness. Her bond with Colin was drawing her out of her shell a little bit. Honestly, though, I agreed with her. I hoped Tobias suffered.

Colin came to check on her. "How are you feeling, sunshine?"

She gave him a half smile. "I'm not sure. Can we work on this charging spell and talk about the blinking power later?"

Colin nodded and sat beside her, leaning forward to kiss her forehead. "Of course."

I went back into the kitchen with Luca and started working on the new spell for a healing remedy while we waited for Neva and Cyrus to get back from Barnaby's.

Chapter Eleven

Tuesday, June 27, 2023

Izzy

As I tried to forget about the blinking situation, Colin's phone beeped with a text from Celeste. "What did she say?"

Colin turned his phone so I could read her message.

Meeting tonight at 7 p.m. at the GWP. We have new evidence as well as a verified location of the rift the demon is coming through. Bring the girls with you. They need to hear this too.

"Wow. Paxton must have been able to get quite a bit of information out of Maggie and Beth already."

Colin nodded and slipped his phone back into his pocket. "Yeah. Seems that way. Let's finish this charging spell and grab something to eat before we go."

———— ◎ ————

Colin, Sadie, Luca, and I arrived at the GWP ten minutes early and found our seats toward the front of the large room. Neva, Mel, and Donald sat in the row directly behind us. The seats were just about filled when Celeste came in from the back room. The room went quiet when she stepped up to the podium.

"Thank you all so much for coming tonight," she said, her beautiful Scottish accent filling the room. "I apologize for the short notice, but this meeting involves something that could affect us all, so I'll get right to it. The man we believe killed Rosie and Raymond Craig made a huge mistake when he allowed Sadie Craig to see his true form. After twenty-one years of searching for Rosie's killer, we discovered we were looking in the wrong place. We apprehended two young ladies last night who have been working for the man as well as a warlock he hired. They verified that this man is, in fact, a demon."

Gasps filled the room, and Celeste raised her hand to silence everyone.

"We have thought for so long that demons couldn't come to our realm, but we were very wrong. There is a rift between the Bean & Bake and Enchanted Scoops that opens every twenty-one years. It only stays open for sixty days. It is not visible until someone comes through it, so we were unaware.

"The demon's realm has a lunar cycle of thirty days, but we assume their days are twice as long as ours since we know he was the one spotted outside Roots & Remedies in mid-May. That rift has been open since at least then. Once their moon shifts to a new lunar cycle, the rift will close for another twenty-one years. Because of this new information, we managed to pinpoint where the ley lines cross and the locations other possible rifts, but we are unsure of where they open up to.

"Elliott and Elijah are almost finished designing a sensor to put in the alleyway so we will know when the rift is being used. One of our own unbound familiars has volunteered to make contact with the demon and see exactly what he wants and is planning to do. We already know that he seeks the Hazel Craig spell book, but we don't know what he plans to do with it. Luca Matthews and Colin Jacobs were pulled into that realm a while back, so we do have a little information from that.

"Until further notice, everyone is to stay out of the alley. Donald and Mel have agreed to let the residents in the upstairs apartments use the inside stairway so they can avoid the alley as well. Someone will be monitoring the area at all hours as well as watching the sensor feedback. If you see anything at all suspicious, please use your alarms to contact us, and we will look into it.

"That is all the information we have at this time, but please, keep an eye on your GWP messages for further updates and sightings. Does anyone have any questions?"

The room was silent for a few moments.

"Please be aware of the happenings in this town. We don't want any more murders to occur because of this." Celeste gave the room a slight nod. "You're all dismissed."

As the room cleared, Celeste asked the seven of us to stay for a few more minutes. We moved to a large table behind the podium, and Celeste sat at its head. Thoughts filled my mind of everything that could possibly go wrong. *What if Sadie and I can't learn our powers before Tobias returns? How are we supposed to learn how to use so many powers all at once?*

Colin must have realized I was in a daze because he took my hand and placed a warm kiss on the top of it. *"Don't worry, sunshine. We're here with you. We'll be with you every step of the way."*

I smiled and placed my head against his arm. *"I know. It's just a bit overwhelming."*

He kissed the top of my head. *"It is. But we'll keep you safe. I promise."*

Celeste made eye contact with Mel. "We think you were thrown against the alley wall the other day because you got too close to the rift. Thankfully, you're okay, so we just need you to avoid the alley until we can close the gateway."

Mel nodded and glanced at Donald. "We can do that. We have a few extra trash cans, and I'm sure we can use Marissa's dumpster at Enchanted Scoops." She smiled at Celeste. "I'm under doctor's orders to take it easy for at least another week, so I can keep an eye on the monitors Elliott and Elijah install."

Celeste nodded. "Thank you. They will show you how it works. Everything will be monitored at the GWP as well by Tyson, but he may get behind, so if you notice any spikes in activity, be sure to let him know right away."

"Will do," Mel said as she gripped Donald's arm.

"Luca and Colin. I need you two to start working with the girls on their elemental powers. I'll contact Felix tonight and send him to help you work with them since you don't have the powers yourselves."

Luca and Colin agreed, and Celeste looked at me and Sadie.

"Raymond believed you both have all five elemental powers. You may find it helpful to split them and learn two each until you can perfect them all. The spirit elemental power comes to you in time, so you don't need to do anything for that one."

A wave of relief went through me knowing that we didn't need to learn them all at once. The spells, self-defense training, running the shop, and developing our powers was all so overwhelming. I never thought we would be so busy when taking over Roots & Remedies. I glanced at my hands then back up at Celeste. "Do any two work together better than the others?"

"Most people have been known to wield either fire and water or air and earth together. Maybe you can split them like that. Then, over time, you can learn them all."

I smiled at Sadie. "You can take fire and water since you had that run-in with the birthday candle when you were younger. I'll take air and earth since I apparently have the air power."

Sadie agreed.

Celeste thanked us for staying and told us to be careful, then we all headed home.

Chapter Twelve
Wednesday, June 28, 2023

Izzy

Around lunchtime, Neva arrived at the shop with Simba and Cyrus. Neva set the carrier on the floor by the bathroom door so he could smell his litter box. The Garfield-sized cat jumped out of his carrier and climbed into it. He gently dug around the box then climbed back out to his bed in the front room and jumped up into the windowsill and sniffed at Luca.

"Why are you looking at me like that, Simba? Binx didn't sleep in your bed." Luca walked toward him.

Approaching the cat in the window, I squatted to his level to pet his head. "Simba, what's wrong?"

"*Nothing. He can lie in my bed instead of beside it,*" he replied as he looked up at Luca.

I turned to Luca and Sadie. "Um. Simba said that Binx could have slept in his bed."Luca furrowed his brow and glanced toward Colin. "Your lasagna buddy is much more thoughtful than Garfield would be. He never let Odie in his bed."

I laughed and scratched Simba's cheek.

Sadie glanced at me with a furrowed brow. "What's so funny?" Her eyes shifted back toward Colin as he approached.

"Simba said he prefers alfredo," I explained. "Tomato sauce gives him a bellyache."

"Ha. I can relate. We can order some for lunch if you're hungry, Simba." Colin rubbed the cat's head.

Simba walked in a circle and sat on his bed, giving Colin a quiet meow as if agreeing to the lunch plan.

We walked back into the kitchen, where Neva and Cyrus were processing some of the herbs Sadie had taken out of the dehydrator a few minutes earlier.

"So, can you talk to Simba yet?" Neva asked Sadie as they sat at the island.

"I can talk to him, and he seems to understand me, but I can't understand him. I just hear meows back. But Izzy can understand him. I thought animals had a universal language."

Cyrus nodded. "They do for the most part. But they communicate over several different frequencies. That's probably why you can't hear him but Izzy can."

I squeezed onto the stool beside Neva at the island. "Simba said he prefers alfredo instead of lasagna. We were going to order lunch from Tastes of Italian down the street. Can he have some?"

She smiled. "Yes, just make his a kid's portion. Cyrus and I can pick it up when it's ready."

———————— ◉ ————————

After we ate, I watched as Simba washed his paws and face.

"So, how was your alfredo, Simba?" I asked.

"*It was good. I'm going to sleep like Garfield now.*" Jumping down, he headed to his bed in the front window of the shop.

I watched him as he spun around and got comfortable. Simba had such a simple life. It made me a little jealous.

"*What do you guys do when you aren't bonded or on assignment? Are you able to live like Simba?*" I asked Colin telepathically.

"*That is a very odd question. What made you want to know?*" he asked.

"*I want to learn more about becoming a familiar. I have a feeling that I won't be able to accomplish everything I want in my lifetime, so if I can become a familiar, even if I never bind, I can possibly accomplish those things. And it would be nice being able to turn into a cat and sleep in weird positions.*"

"*Sleeping in weird positions isn't all it's cracked up to be. But I understand wanting to accomplish so much. Let's get you trained on all your powers first then find and destroy Hazel's spell book. I promise I'll explain the process after that.*" He peeked into the front room at me from where he stood at the island with Luca and Cyrus.

I smiled and blew him a kiss, and he pretended to catch it and put it in his pocket before turning back to his conversation with them.

I giggled and sat at my desk to go through the piles of stones and beads that Neva and Cyrus had picked up from Barnaby's for us. The new life that Sadie and I were thrown into was definitely hectic, but it was starting to develop a bit of normalcy, and I was glad to have Colin, Sadie, and Luca by my side through it all.

Chapter Thirteen

Thursday, June 29, 2023

Sadie

We spent a couple of hours working on different punching and blocking techniques that we might face in the battle with Tobias. Luca and Colin showed us some martial arts moves, and we caught on quickly to those as well.

As I leaned against the wall by the bathroom after practice, waiting for Izzy to change into her regular clothes, I closed my eyes for a minute to clear my mind, but as I focused on my breathing, flashes of a vision continued to disrupt my attempt. All I could see was a lady coming into the shop, asking for an obsidian pendent with a specific sigil carved into it.

"Sadie, you can go in now." Izzy nudged my arm.

"Huh?"

"You can use the bathroom now. Are you okay?"

"Yeah, why wouldn't I be?" I entered the bathroom and closed the door behind me. The image of the lady in her mid-fifties with short, curly hair popped into my head again as I closed my eyes to pull my shirt over my head. It looked as if Izzy was handing her the obsidian stone. The carved sigil had been filled in with a metallic silver paint.

Someone knocked at the bathroom door. "Are you okay in there?" Izzy asked.

"Yeah, I'll be right out." I finished changing, and when I came out, Izzy, Colin, and Luca were waiting at the door to the stairway. "Can you carve sigils into obsidian stones to make them more powerful?"

Luca appeared confused. "Um. I don't know. Why do you ask?"

"An image of one came to me a few minutes ago, and I was curious."

We headed downstairs and thanked Neva and Cyrus for watching the shop. They got Simba into his carrier and headed out the kitchen door. Izzy and I sat at our desks with Luca and Colin to work on some of the spells Pops had in his journals.

About thirty minutes later, the bell over the door rang, letting us know someone was coming into the shop. I closed my journal, and as I looked up, my jaw dropped. It was the lady from the visions in my head earlier. She started peering in the jewelry cases up against Izzy's desk.

Izzy walked around to the back of the jewelry case where the lady stood. "Can I help you with anything?"

The lady smiled up at her. "I doubt you have what I'm looking for. No one in a fifty-mile radius has had it."

"May I ask what that is, ma'am?" Izzy asked.

"I just moved to this area, and I've recently gotten out of a dangerous relationship. I wanted to get a pendent made of obsidian, but I wanted a sigil carved into it for extra protection."

Izzy, Luca, and Colin all looked at me, shocked. I walked to the counter beside Izzy and smiled at the lady. "We don't have anything like that, but I'm sure Izzy can make one for you. Would you like the sigil to be painted as well? Maybe a metallic silver?"

Her eyes went wide. "Oh, my lovelies. Could you really do that? I will pay whatever you want plus some if you can do that."

I gave her a quick nod. "Since we have to make the item specifically, it will take us about a week."

"That would be perfect. I have a friend who lives in Shawsville that I can stay with until it's ready." She dug through her purse, pulled out a piece of paper, unfolded it, and laid it on the counter. "This is the sigil I'd like to have carved into it, if it's not too hard."

I grabbed the pen from the top of Izzy's desk. "Can you write down your name and number? We'll call you when it's ready."

She jotted down her information. "You ladies have made me feel like I might have a chance at being safe again. Thank you so much."

"You are very welcome, Ms. Ambrose. We will be in touch."

Once she was out the door, Izzy elbowed me in the arm.

"Ouch! What was that for?" I rubbed the spot where her elbow made contact.

"I don't know how to carve sigils into stones. Why did you tell her I could?" Izzy's face reddened.

"Is this why you asked if sigils could be carved into the stones when we were upstairs?" Luca asked.

"Yes. While I was waiting for Izzy to finish in the bathroom, I closed my eyes to clear my mind, and I watched that exact scene of her coming in play out in my mind. When I was inside the bathroom changing, I closed my eyes again to pull my shirt over my head, and I saw her come back in wearing different clothes than today. Izzy handed her the obsidian stone with a sigil carved into it that was filled in with metallic silver paint."

"And why do you think I can actually go through with it?" Izzy rubbed her temples.

"Because Pops always said you could do anything you put your mind to, and I know he's right. It might take a couple of tries, but I think you can do it." I leaned in to put my head against hers. "You just have to believe in yourself, Daisy."

She smiled at me. "You had to go and call me Daisy, didn't you? I'll see what I can find out about carving into stones."

"Pops would be proud," I said with a crooked smile.

She rolled her eyes at me for using Pops's nickname for her because I knew she wouldn't be able to refuse me if I did. Then she walked around to sit back down at her desk.

The guys stood beside Izzy, watching me as I walked to my desk to sit down.

"What?" I asked.

"I think you have the power of premonition." Luca glanced at Colin. "If so, we might actually be okay when Tobias shows up." Luca walked over and kissed the top of my head. "You just added more training to your schedule, though."

We closed the shop at half past five and headed over to Plum's Hardware. Izzy had found some YouTube videos on how to carve designs into stones. Ruthie Plum was at the register when we went inside. We told her what we were looking for, and she showed us where the Dremels and bits were located. She insisted that Izzy get some protective eyewear and gloves and even a respirator mask so she wouldn't breathe in the dust. Once we had everything we needed, we headed up to the register.

Once we got home, Izzy watched more videos on safety and laying out the designs. Colin was by her side the entire time, saying that he would be there with her every step of the way. Izzy still had some timidness about her since binding with Colin, but she was slowly coming out of her shell and trying things.

If I hadn't had the second vision of Ms. Ambrose coming back in to pick up the stone, I wouldn't have pushed Izzy to try it. I wasn't sure what my visions were trying to tell me, but I had to be seeing them for a reason.

Chapter Fourteen
Thursday, June 29, 2023

Sadie

We were busy most of the morning and had sold out of our poison ivy salve. The group of guys from the local landscaping company that had been given the challenge to clear the poison ivy from the elementary school playground had cleaned us out.

I headed back into the kitchen to start a couple of batches of salve. The landscapers had mentioned that at least an acre of poison ivy needed to be pulled. They expected to be even itchier by the end of the day, so I told them I would make more, just in case.

At a quarter to noon, Cyrus and Neva entered the store through the kitchen door. Izzy finished with the customer that had come in to place an order for an anniversary present for his wife then came into the kitchen, followed by Binx and Smokey. The cats jumped up onto the counter and waited to hear the news from Cyrus's meeting with Tobias.

"How did it go?" Izzy climbed up on the stool beside Neva.

Cyrus took a deep breath. "Well, Izzy's blink was very accurate. He wants me to help him steal the spell book. He said he has someone else on the inside, but he wouldn't tell me who it was. We all need to be very careful with what we say to anyone at the GWP."

"Did you agree to help him?" I asked as I placed the glass bowl over the boiling water on the stove.

"He said to meet him at the rift in the alley in three days if I agree to help, and he will take me to Demoria. He promised to give me powers and make me immortal if we succeed in getting the spell book."

"Aren't you already immortal?" Izzy furrowed her brow.

"Yes and no. I can still be killed, but I won't die from natural causes since I'm an unbound familiar," he said.

"Did he tell you anything about his plan yet?" I asked.

Cyrus shook his head. "Nothing aside from wanting me to help him steal the book. I won't learn more details until I meet him in his realm."

"The device that Elliott and Elijah made caught the energy signature of the rift when Tobias came through it this morning. At least we will know when someone passes through it now," Neva said as she rubbed Cyrus's arm.

"Were you at the GWP when Tobias went through it?" Izzy asked.

She gave Izzy a quick nod. "Yeah, I was helping watch the cameras they set up in the alley. Unfortunately, Tobias didn't use his powers while he was in that area, so we didn't get an energy signature on his individual powers. We will be going in blind on that part."

"I'll check in as often as I can once I find out more from going to Demoria," Cyrus said as he took Neva's hand.

It seemed as if the fake-boyfriend-and-girlfriend assignment was forming some true connection between them.

I poured the salve mixture into the jars, and once I finished, I wiped out the remaining oil residue with a paper towel before putting the bowl in the sink. We talked for another five minutes before a customer came in.

Neva and Cyrus left for the GWP a few minutes later to work on a way for Cyrus to contact us from Demoria. I hated that he would be cut off from our realm, but he kept telling us that he would be okay. I just hoped he came back in one piece.

After lunch, Izzy and Colin were at the table in the greenhouse, working on trying to carve a sigil into a rock Colin had found in the parking lot. Izzy wanted to practice on a regular rock before trying with the obsidian stone.

Luca and I were working on a mixture for a stronger healing salve. I had crushed the dry herbs in the mortar and pestle and was melting down the coconut oil in the double boiler. As I stirred in the other liquid ingredients, Luca handed me the mortar with the herbs, and I mixed them in as well.

I felt a yawn coming on, and when my eyes closed, I saw a flash of a sigil drawn into the herbs floating on top of the mixture. When I processed what I had seen, I went to the drawer where I kept the spoons and spatulas. I dug through the drawer and found a wooden bamboo kebab skewer.

When I glanced at Luca, he seemed to be trying to figure out what I was doing. I took the glass bowl off the pan of boiling water and placed it on the counter. I added the herbs while stirring the mixture and waited a few minutes before using the skewer to draw the sigil into the melted salve. As I finished connecting the circle around the outside, the sigil glowed a faint purple color. I gave Luca a cheeky grin.

He looked from me to the mixture then back to me again. "Um. I'm impressed. How did you know that would do anything?" His brow rose.

"I had a premonition of the sigil glowing in the warm salve. I figured it was a sign to try it." I poured the salve into the jars, and when I turned to grab a paper towel to wipe out the bowl, Luca was still staring at me. "What?"

He smiled and shook his head. "You are full of surprises."

He kissed me on the cheek, and when I turned to him, I was caught in his magnetic gaze. The butterflies in my belly that had been calm for the last few days started to flutter, and heat rose in my cheeks.

Izzy walked into the kitchen and stopped when she saw us.

I forced my eyes closed to break our gaze, cleared my throat, and turned to Izzy. "Hey, Izzy. I had another premonition, this one showing someone drawing a sigil into the melted salve mixture."

She glanced at Luca then smiled at me. "Oh yeah? Did you try it?"

"I did, and the sigil glowed a faint purple before disappearing."

Her eyes kept shifting between me and Luca, and I knew what was going through her head.

"Do you know what it does to the salve?"

I shook my head. "Not for sure. Since I'm working on a healing salve, I assume it will strengthen it so you heal faster. I won't know until one of us needs it."

She grabbed two bottles of water from the fridge. "Well, hopefully it works. It will be nice if we can strengthen any healing aid. I'll let you two get back to it." She winked at me and headed out to the greenhouse with Colin.

Chapter Fifteen
Thursday, June 29, 2023

Izzy

"You just have to keep in mind that obsidian is a much harder material than this rock. You may have to concentrate on one spot a bit longer than with this one." Colin rolled the obsidian stone in his hand, his eyes lingering on the gravel I'd practiced on.

I had searched for an obsidian stone to wrap that had more of a flat spot so the sigil could sit flush. I happened to find the perfect one. It was shaped like a skipping stone but a bit thicker.

Colin handed me the stone with the sigil drawn on it in silver pen. I put my glove back on my left hand so I wouldn't get injured, but due to the stone's size and slickness, every time I placed the engraving tip to the stone, it slid out of my grip. Taking off the glove, I kept my fingers away from the tip of the engraver as I tried again. I got the inside of the sigil completed, and as I carved the circle around it, the tip kicked. It startled me, and I jerked the engraver away from the stone. Taking a deep breath, I started at the same spot, but it kicked again, and the tip of the engraver went right into the tip of my pointer finger.

I gasped and dropped the engraver onto the table and wrapped my hand around my finger. Colin grabbed the Dremel and turned it off then ran into the kitchen to get a clean rag.

He came back out to the greenhouse and wrapped the towel around my finger. "Here, squeeze this to keep the bleeding down, and hold your hand up like this." He moved my hands up to my chest and guided me into the bathroom then turned on the water and started gently unwrapping the rag from my finger.

Sadie came in to see what had happened. "Um. I wanted to try out my new salve, but you didn't have to cut yourself that quickly."

"Oh, trust me. I wouldn't have done this on purpose. It hurts so bad. I can feel my heartbeat in my finger." I winced when the cold water hit my finger. After a few seconds, the pain was a little more bearable. "I guess you can try some of your healing salve on it. I don't think my healing sigil tattoo will help too much. This cut needs more than that. I've got a chunk missing."

She grabbed the jar of salve from the kitchen and the first aid kit from the linen closet. She pulled out a tongue depressor and dipped it into the salve and scooped out a gob. "This cut is pretty deep, so this might burn."

I grabbed my left wrist with my right hand to steady it and closed my eyes. Colin turned the water off and dried my finger around the cut, then opened a new gauze. Sadie put the gob of salve on my finger, and at first, I didn't feel it. Colin wrapped the gauze around my finger, and it pushed the salve into the cut more. I gasped and squeezed my wrist tighter, wincing again as I turned my head.

I was so mad at myself for taking off the gloves, but it was too late. I would have to find another way to hold onto the stone while carving it.

Colin taped the gauze closed and rested my injured hand against my chest.

I studied the gauze wrapped around my finger. "Do you think Plum's would have anything I could put on the gloves to make them less slippery?"

"I'm not sure, but we can look. We should take the gloves and stone with us. Maybe Wayne or Ruthie will have an idea of something we could try." Colin leaned down and kissed the top of my head. "Let's go see what they have available."

"I need to go to Everything's Crafty, too, for the silver paint. I was thinking about trying the paint used for model cars. My dad and Elliott used to paint theirs. It seems to hold up well."

Colin nodded and went to grab the gloves and stone from the greenhouse while I told Sadie and Luca we were going out.

Wayne Plum was at the front of the store when we went inside. Colin filled him in on what we were looking for, and he took us back to show us some options. We went with the cheapest he suggested and purchased a hot-glue gun with a few glue sticks included. He said I could put hot glue dots or stripes on the fingertips of the glove, and if I was working on a smooth stone, I could hot glue it to the surface then peel the glue off when I was finished. He gave me a three-inch square of plexiglass that I could glue the stone to and still be able to move it around. I paid for the glue gun, and we left to get the paint. I chose two colors of silver, a light and a dark shade, along with a set of tiny brushes and took them to the counter to pay.

We had been gone for maybe thirty minutes, and by the time we got back to Roots & Remedies, my finger had stopped throbbing. I plugged in the hot-glue gun and carefully slid my hand into the glove. Once the glue gun had heated up, I put in a glue stick and drew stripes on the glove's fingertips, then I put a gob of hot glue on the piece of plexiglass and stuck the obsidian stone onto it. Unplugging the glue gun, I let all the glue dry for a few minutes before I tried to finish the sigil.

Colin picked up the piece of plexiglass the stone was glued to and looked at the spot the engraver tip had kicked off. "You might want to start on the other side of the spot that gave you a hard time. It might be the angle of cut that caused it. If you go the other way over that spot, it might not kick too bad."

I nodded and positioned the stone then slowly and carefully started engraving again. After a few minutes of working on it, I got to that spot. Gripping the stone tighter, with my pointer finger in the air, I glided over the rock with no issues. I went over that same point again to smooth the cut. When I set down the stone so I could change tips on the Dremel, the sigil glowed a faint reddish color for a few seconds before fading.

"Colin, is it supposed to do that?" I asked with wide eyes.

"I don't know. I've never seen a stone or crystal done like this. I've seen people do it with runes but not these." He shrugged. "I guess I've seen it now."

I switched to the buffing bit and buffed the groove to remove any sharp spots. By the time I went to take off my gloves, I had forgotten about the cut on my finger, and as I pulled out my hand, the bandage stuck inside the glove. Colin gasped and grabbed my hand, holding it up. We both looked at it, and our eyes widened. The cut was completely closed. It hadn't just sealed itself shut. New skin had grown over it already.

"That would explain why it wasn't hurting anymore," I said.

Colin and I went into the front room, where Sadie sat with Luca, and showed them my finger.

Sadie's eyes went wide, and her jaw dropped. "How in the world is that healed already?" She looked closer and shook her head. "I didn't expect skin to grow back like this. You still have an indent there, though. I wonder if that will even itself out. This is amazing. I can't sell this in here. People will be suspicious if it heals wounds this fast. But maybe it will give us the upper hand against Tobias. Slap some on our wounds and keep fighting."

Chapter Sixteen

Saturday, July 1, 2023

Luca

We headed upstairs with Sadie and Izzy after Neva and Cyrus showed up at a quarter to three. The girls went back to the bathroom to change into their workout clothes, and Colin and I changed into our shorts. Then I had the girls sit on the mats.

"We're going to do something a little different today," I said. "I think we need to work on meditation and relaxation techniques."

Sadie glanced at Izzy then back at me and smiled. "We already know how to do that. I learned that in college."

Colin chuckled. "What you learned at school is a lot different from what you will be learning with us. A lot of your powers will only come to light if you know how to call upon them. From today forward, you will need to meditate at least once a day. It wouldn't hurt to do it in the morning then again at night to calm yourself before bed."

"We know Raymond had the blinking power, but what happened to Izzy the other day went a bit further than just a normal blinking episode. That was more of an interdimensional perception where you could see what was happening in real time. Both powers work the same as far as being able to send your mind somewhere else—which is different from astral projection, the ability to send your physical body to another realm or plane of existence where you can touch and move things."

Sadie looked up at me with confusion. "So, Pops couldn't send his body to another realm? I thought that was how he got you guys out of the realm where you were being tortured."

"Raymond never actually came into that realm," I explained. "He did a spell that pulled us back. He was somehow able to find us in the other realm. We never asked how. We were just grateful that he got us out of there."

Izzy furrowed her brow. "So, how will meditation and relaxation help us with any of this?"

I looked at Sadie. "Do you remember when you were having the dreams about being in Africa and working with the big cats?"

She nodded slowly.

"That was your zoolingualism or spirit power getting stronger. With all the stress of learning about this life, you need to learn the relaxation and meditation techniques to calm your mind and body. This will enhance your ability to grow, even when you're resting."

"So, I guess me floating for a few seconds before I fell off my bed would have been my air powers growing stronger?" Izzy looked from me to Colin.

I nodded. "Yeah, more than likely. We haven't seen any other powers so far that would cause that."

"Okay, so what do we need to do for this meditation?" she asked.

"You need to learn how to relax first. You'll flex each group of muscles then release from there. Are you ready?" Colin asked.

Both girls nodded, and I showed them how to lie down to flex properly.

"Okay, with each muscle group, you will flex slowly three times then relax for five seconds before moving to the next group of muscles. The first part will be your toes."

The girls gave me a surprised look.

"How do we flex our toes?" Sadie wiggled hers back and forth.

I chuckled at the sight of her toes dancing around. "All you have to do is curl them then spread them apart as far as you can. You can alternate between feet as well."

The girls did well with the tightening of each muscle group, then we went into the meditation part of the exercise. That part was harder for Sadie than it was for Izzy. Sadie was quite a bit more fidgety. I moved the girls to face each other and had them hold hands, then had Sadie follow Izzy's breathing. After a few minutes, Sadie finally relaxed enough to where we could start the breathing exercises.

After about ten minutes of that, I explained the dreaming process.

Izzy cut in. "And how are we supposed to guide our dreams?"

I took a deep breath. "When you do your relaxation and meditation exercises before bed, you can guide your dreams by asking for them."

They shot me a puzzled glance.

"CARDS: clarify the issue, ask the question, repeat it, dream and document it, study the dream."

"Clarify, ask, repeat, dream, and study?" Sadie asked. "Is this really supposed to work?"

"It's worked for a lot of people. With paranormals, though, it can help solve problems that we can't figure out otherwise. For example, if you start having trouble writing a spell and you can't figure out what you're missing in the recipe, right before you fall asleep, you could use CARDS to jump-start your mind to be thinking of a solution to the problem."

The girls still seemed confused.

"I'll write it down for you, and you can practice it."

They nodded.

"Okay. Let's get started," I said.

After about fifteen minutes of breathing exercises, we called it quits. I could tell Sadie was struggling to completely clear her mind, but maybe she would catch on faster when she tried it with just Izzy.

"Can we practice some combat stuff before we head back downstairs?" Sadie asked as she and Izzy stood and stretched.

We got into position and exchanged some punches and kicks for about thirty minutes, with the girls blocking every one of them. I was so proud of them with how fast they were catching on to the moves in training. I hated throwing so much at Sadie and Izzy at once, but with everything happening with Tobias and his realm, we had to be prepared. Raymond had told us that he'd instilled in them all the knowledge they would need for their training. I just had to get them to figure out what it was.

We all got changed and went back down to the shop.

Sadie

After dinner, Luca and Colin wanted to work on our air and water powers. Luca and I set up in the kitchen, and Izzy and Colin set up in the living room. Luca set a cookie sheet on the floor and put enough water in it to fill it halfway. He had me sit on the floor in front of it, and he sat across from me, then he reached into his pocket and pulled out a bottle cap and placed it in the water.

He positioned my hands over the cookie sheet, palms down about three inches from the water. "Close your eyes and clear your mind. Once you feel focused, see if you can sense the water's presence without touching it."

I rolled my eyes at the awkwardness of the whole situation that made me feel silly but took a deep breath and closed my eyes to clear my mind. After a couple of minutes, I tried sensing the water under my hands. Then I peeked at Luca, and he raised his brow.

"Keep your eyes closed and focus," he said. "Try to connect with its energy and create a link to it."

I was focusing as hard as I could, but I had never really been good at clearing my mind. While learning meditation in college, I had gone to bed feeling more stressed afterward. "Luca, I really can't sense the water."

"Shh. Imagine the water is steaming and that your hands are absorbing the moisture, but instead of it being hot, it feels very cool. Once you connect with the water, you will be able to control it just like you control your energy."

A few more minutes went by, and I started to get a headache. "Luca, I don't think this is working. I can't feel the water."

"Close your eyes and try again. Once you get this part down, you'll be able to make the water move."

I began to feel more impatient than normal. Luca's directions weren't working. Maybe I wasn't meant to have water power. I didn't remember having anything unexplainable happen with water when I was younger. *Why did Pops think I have water power?*

I closed my eyes and tried again. After about five minutes of silence, my patience was up, and I looked at Luca. "This isn't working." I lifted my hands to slam them into the water but stopped about three inches away. The water started to slosh around the cookie sheet like I had actually slammed my hands into it. "How did I do that?"

Luca smirked. "Did you feel the water?"

I shook my head. "No, not until it splashed onto my hand just now."

"Maybe you felt it but didn't realize that was what it was."

"I didn't feel anything, and I have no idea how I made the water move. Maybe I hit it with my leg." I took a deep breath. "I'm sorry.

That came out mean. I just don't know how I did it. Maybe this isn't an element I can control."

"Raymond thought you could. He hasn't been wrong about any of your powers yet." Luca stood and picked up the cookie sheet to dump the water into the sink. "We can try again tomorrow. It will be a long day. We should get some sleep."

Izzy

"So, when you used your air power the other day and we hit the mats, that was from you inhaling the air. You will need to learn to control that part, too, but what we'll work on today is controlling the air with your hands," Colin said as he pushed the coffee table out of the way.

"Oh, will these be moves like the air bender dude uses in the movies?" I asked, hyping myself up to learn yet another skill.

Colin raised an eyebrow at me. "We'll learn that, but right now, we can start on a much smaller scale. Are you ready?"

I nodded, and he gestured for me to sit on the couch beside him. "Hold your hands with your palms facing each other, like this, and bring them about three inches from your face."

I put my hands up like he had his. "Okay. Got it."

"Clear your mind." He waited about a minute. "Now, blow a steady stream of air between your palms, and move your right hand to push the air into your left hand, kinda like you're tossing a small ball back and forth. It might take a few tries before you feel the force hit your left hand." He showed me how to do it then turned to watch me.

I took a deep breath and released the air as steadily as I could, moving my right hand toward my left hand simultaneously. Then I moved my left hand toward my right hand and continued back and forth. I did this for about a minute before I put my hands back down. "Colin, I don't feel anything, and I'm getting lightheaded from breathing like this."

"Take a minute, then we can try blowing air into your cupped hand instead."

I nodded, and when I was ready, I took my position again, cupping my hands this time. I tried it that way for another minute, blowing air into my hands every other time. "I'm not feeling any force with this." I flung my hands in aggravation, and the papers on the table moved. "Oh geez. I swear I didn't feel that."

"It's okay. It will take some time to learn the spells and skills. You don't have to know them all at once." He leaned in and kissed my cheek.

"I know, but Tobias will be here soon. How will I learn to wield the powers of air and earth, plus help Sadie keep the shop up and running, practice my spells, and develop all these new powers popping up? Plus, I haven't had any time to do my drawings or paint, and I don't want to forget about my passions." I wrapped my arms around myself and lay back on the couch.

Colin scooted back and pulled me to him. "I know it seems like a lot, but look at how quickly you and Sadie caught on to the defensive training and the spells Raymond left for you in his packages."

I shrugged as Sadie and Luca came into the living room. "How did it go with you, Sadie?"

She rolled her eyes and plopped onto the love seat with Luca. "I made it move, but I couldn't *feel* it."

"Ha, that sounds like me. I made the papers move by apparently throwing a ball of air that way, but I didn't feel it."

"You'll catch on before you know it." Colin pushed a strand of hair out of my face. "It's a lot of information to absorb. Just like everything you've worked on over the years, like your remedies and your art, you didn't learn it overnight."

"I know, but with that, we didn't have the threat of someone evil coming to steal anything from us," I said.

"You have the entire GWP behind you to stand against Tobias. You aren't in this alone." Colin rubbed my shoulder.

"I wish Pops or our parents had told us about this world sooner. I think we would have had a better understanding of things," Sadie said.

"Raymond has been working with you girls since you were little to prepare you without telling you. You both seem to be struggling with the relaxation and meditation stuff, but I'm pretty sure Raymond instilled something in you without you knowing it. If you can figure out what that is and learn to relax and meditate fully, you will definitely notice the difference." Luca pulled Sadie closer to him and kissed the top of her head.

Sadie and I tried to remember back to when we were little and the things we did with Pops that could have been to help us relax, but we couldn't think of anything. I lay in bed for another hour, trying to think about what Pops could have taught us about calming ourselves and came up blank. I even used the CARDS technique to see if my dreams would reveal what it could be. But that, too, failed.

Chapter Seventeen

Sunday, July 2, 2023

Izzy

We arrived at the GWP's arena at seven in the morning to beat the heat. We wanted to be home by two that afternoon to relax before getting ready for the meeting at the GWP at seven.

"Hello, ladies. My name is Felix. I will be helping Luca and Colin train you to wield the elements. Have you had any luck as of yet?" he asked as he set a box on the bench beside us.

He was a short, thin man with gray hair and a mustache—not what I expected a teacher of the elements to look like. He reminded me of someone who would sit behind a desk and do taxes or some other office-related job.

"I made some papers move, and Sadie made the water move, but neither of us could sense the power." I pulled my jacket closer around me as a big breeze swept across the arena. I seemed to be the only one who reacted to it.

He furrowed his brow and nodded. "Sometimes relaxing can help that, but at least you were able to move it. How did you feel when that happened?"

Sadie's eyes widened. "I was aggravated."

"So was I." I shivered again as the breeze came from the opposite direction and sent chills through my body.

"That makes sense. Your power will feed off your mood. Your level of relaxation will help you control it." Felix pulled a few things from his bag.

That would explain why we couldn't feel it. I thought I felt less overwhelmed after meditating at night, but maybe I wasn't clearing my mind enough.

Next, Felix brought materials from the storage shed beside the main building and set up what looked to be different obstacles. He walked back over to get one more thing from his box. "I'm only here for one day, so we have a lot to cover in six hours. Since you aren't feeling the force of your powers, I will give you the basics of how to use them. As you learn to properly meditate, Luca and Colin will be able to help you control the elements better."

Sadie and I nodded and followed him to the first area he had set up, where a ball rested on top of a stand.

"I was informed that you both possess at least two elemental powers," Felix said. "I'd like you to try each course. These powers are rare—let alone possessing more than one."

"Okay, what do we need to do?" I studied the stand five feet in front of us.

"I apologize ahead of time for this, but I need to make you mad. I don't know the details of your situation aside from that you're facing a powerful demon. Have you seen his face?" he asked.

"Sadie has seen him a couple of times in person. I've only seen him when I blinked." I took a deep breath as the image of Tobias popped into my head.

Felix gave a quick nod. "Which one of you is supposed to have the air power?"

I stepped forward. "That would be me."

"I want you to picture that the ball in front of you is his face. I'll show you the movements to copy, and I want you to imagine the air you are whirling around will hit him." He crossed his wrists in front of him at his waist. He moved his arms swiftly in opposite directions as if to draw a circle in the air then clasped his hands at the top and slowly brought them down to his chest. He stood like that for about three seconds with his eyes closed then shoved his hands forward.

The ball on the stand went flying forward, and Luca ran to get it. He returned the ball to the stand, and Felix gestured for me to try it.

I took a deep breath and crossed my arms in front of me. I followed his steps, and when I pushed forward from my chest, the ball didn't move. "Did I do it right?"

"Yes and no. I should have specified the breathing part. Take a deep breath in as you go around and hold it. When you push forward, release it all at once."

I tried again, and the ball moved a tiny bit but didn't fall.

Felix gestured for me to do it again. "This time, I want you to think about why this demon makes you mad."

I nodded, and when I clasped my hands, I thought of my devastation when I saw those police cars at Roots & Remedies. When I pushed forward, the ball rolled off the stand but didn't go far.

Felix had Sadie try it three times, but nothing happened for her.

He then took us to a barrel full of water. "Which one of you is supposed to have the water power?"

Sadie stepped up beside him and waited for his instructions. "I want you to imagine you are in the middle of the battle and this demon is running toward you with a torch. You need to defend yourself. You need to move the water from that barrel to put out the torch so he can't burn you. To do this, you need to locate your water source, reach toward it, and close your hand around it as if it were the end of a rope, then throw it at the target. Inhale as you reach back, and exhale when you throw the water."

She nodded and got into position, reaching for the water behind her right side. She inhaled while reaching back toward the barrel, closed her hand, and quickly swung her arm forward as if to hit someone. The water in the barrel sloshed around but didn't come out.

Felix nodded and gestured for her to do it again. "This time, I want you to imagine he's taunting you about taking what he's after and saying that he's not sorry for what he's done."

Sadie nodded and did it again. A stream of water cascaded out of the barrel, landing about three feet away. Felix gestured for me to try, but the water didn't move at all for me, so we moved onto the fire power.

Sadie stepped up without him asking since the log had a set of matches on it. A candle occupied the center with five more candles standing around it. Felix squatted in front of the log and lit the candle in the center then put his hands on the outside of the candles. "For this one, pretend this center candle is the demon, and you want the fire to spread. You will want to focus on making the flame big enough to light the candles around it."

Sadie nodded and got on her knees in front of the log. "Does my breathing affect this one?"

"No, but you might hold your breath while making the fire bigger, so keep that in mind," he said.

Sadie stretched out her hands and closed her eyes. After about ten seconds, the flame sparked but didn't get any bigger. She took a deep breath and tried again. The flame grew enough to light one of the other candles but not the other four.

When it was my turn, nothing happened, so we went to the final course with an English ivy plant sitting on a log.

"You can both try this one at the same time. You both likely have this power. Normally, if you can control multiple elements, this is one. Since you are new at this, you will want to take off your shoes so you can call the power to you better. After you learn to control the earth, shoes won't make a difference."

Sadie and I removed our shoes and stood on opposite sides of the ivy plant.

"Stand with your feet apart and your palms forward toward the plant. You need steady breaths, and you want to will the plant to move toward your palms. The plant will reach for you, and once it's touching you, you can make it do things like trip someone or bind them. Just keep in mind, a plant this size will only be so strong. Most people with this power call upon vines to bind people."

We took our stances, and I closed my eyes. The ground beneath my feet was cool, but I wiggled my toes deeper into the soft grass. I focused on willing the ivy to reach out to me, and I opened my eyes to focus on a particular hanging strand.

Felix walked a little closer and whispered, "Imagine the ivy reaching out to trip the demon coming toward you."

Once I had the image in my head, the ivy twitched then turned but didn't do anything else. I could see a strand of it heading toward Sadie's hand, but it stopped about an inch away.

Felix clapped, and Sadie and I both looked at him. "Just as I thought. It seems as if you both have the earth power."

Sadie released a big sigh. "Great, another power I have to learn how to control."

Felix put his hand on her shoulder. "Once you figure out how to clear your mind, you will catch on quickly. I will give you instructions on how to wield the elements in several different ways. Luca, Colin, will you two take notes for them?"

They nodded and opened the notes app on their phones so we could sync them all later.

After two more hours of instruction from Felix, he started packing up his box. We helped him move the stuff back to the storage shed and thanked him for his help. He had planned to help us more, but since we hadn't been able to fully clear our minds, he gave us the instructions to follow later. We weren't any closer to wielding the elements, and unless we figured out how to relax completely, we wouldn't be moving along further.

Sadie

We arrived home at quarter to one, and Izzy and I lay down to take a nap so we would hopefully feel better for the meeting with the GWP. Luca woke me at four so I could get a quick shower since it always took me longer to do my hair.

We were all ready by five thirty and decided to get something light to eat before the meeting. We drove to the small diner behind Salem's local car rental and parked. The parking lot was fairly full, but it didn't seem as if many people were inside.

After we ate, we sat and talked about things we had done with Pops as kids, searching for any meaning behind those activities that might help us now. We still hadn't gotten any closer to an answer by the time we needed to leave for the meeting.

Luca parked behind the GWP, and we walked around to the front of the building. Once inside, the secretary pointed us to the elevators and told us everyone was already waiting. We scanned our rings and took the elevator to the sixth floor, where the conference room was located.

Celeste started the meeting by having everyone stand and introduce themselves and say what they did at the GWP.

I tried to do a head count, but before I could finish, Luca leaned in and whispered, "Forty-two plus the four of us."

I flashed him a smile and turned back to the person talking. After the introductions, Celeste went over everything we knew and established the plan. She asked if anyone had ideas that would help, and a few people commented.

The plan seemed pretty straightforward. The night before Tobias was supposed to arrive, people would be scattered throughout town to keep watch. They would call in guards from Richmond and the surrounding areas to assist, and they intended to contain the fight on Main Street when they first wave came through the rift. Containment spells would already be active to keep the damage minimal. Everyone in the room seemed to agree. Celeste ended the meeting answering questions and telling everyone to be safe going home and in the coming days before she pulled Izzy and me aside.

After the final people had left the table to wait in line at the elevators, Celeste pulled out a large box with sigils painted all over it.

She handed it to me and leaned closer to whisper, "I need everyone here to think you have the spell book. Someone in our midst is relaying information to Tobias, but I'm not sure who. Raymond cloaked the book in this box to look like the Craig spell book."

I turned slightly so the people leaving the room could see the box. I heard a few faint gasps but kept my attention on Celeste.

Once the crowd had departed via the elevators, Celeste walked us down to the main floor and had two security guards escort us to my car. Our parents followed us to the parking lot then to the house.

We ordered a couple of pizzas and wings, and we filled our parents in on what had happened since we last saw them. After the pizza arrived, we talked to them about what training they knew Pops did with us when we were younger. Nothing they mentioned would help us with our relaxation issues.

"You know, you could always go visit Pops and hope for some inspiration." My mom tilted her head and raised her eyebrows like she did when we were little and she was trying to convince us to do things.

"You mean go to the cemetery?" Izzy asked.

My mom nodded and took a bite of pizza.

I looked at Izzy. "I guess it can't hurt."

Izzy nodded. "Maybe something will jog our memory when we visit him and Grams. Pops always had stories about Grams when we went to see her. This time, we might remember one about him. We can go during our lunch break tomorrow."

We finished eating, and our parents left shortly after. We got ready for bed, and the guys stayed up to work on a training schedule for us with the notes they got from Felix.

Chapter Eighteen

Monday, July 3, 2023

Izzy

"I don't understand how I'm supposed to wield my earth power. I can't even keep a basic house plant alive." I sat at my desk, gently twirling a strand of English ivy around my finger.

"Maybe once you can control the power better, you can keep them alive." Sadie stroked the ivy's leaves.

"Yeah, maybe. Do you think visiting Pops is going to do any good?"

She shrugged and walked around to sit at her desk. "I'm not sure. I wanna go see him and Grams anyways, so what's the harm?"

I nodded and unwrapped the ivy from my finger then picked up the obsidian stone that I had carved the sigil into and began wrapping the wire around it. "Can you call Ms. Ambrose and let her know she can pick this up this afternoon?"

"Sure." Sadie collected the paper with Ms. Ambrose's information from beside the register to leave her a voice message.

I finished the wrap on the obsidian stone and went to stand at the front window where Smokey was sitting. We watched as the residents went in and out of the stores.

I turned to look toward Sadie. "How can we keep all these nonparanormal people away from Main Street when Tobias shows up? I don't want anyone to get hurt."

She walked to the window where Binx sat and scratched his head as she peered out the window. "I'm not sure. I didn't think to ask Celeste at the meeting."

"*Paranormals will put up glamours throughout town,*" Smokey said telepathically to me.

I glanced down at him. "I guess that makes sense." I looked up at Sadie. "Smokey said they will put up glamours."

"Oh good," Sadie said with relief as she raised her brows then turned to walk back to her desk.

A few minutes later, Neva and Cyrus came in through the kitchen door to watch the shop for us for a couple of hours while we went to the cemetery to visit Pops and Grams. I filled them in on the lady possibly stopping by to pick up the sigil pendant and showed her which chains she could pick from if she wanted one with it.

As we walked to the cemetery at the opposite end of Main Street, Sadie finally broke the silence. "So, is Cyrus ready to go to Demoria tomorrow to meet Tobias?" she asked Luca and Colin.

"As ready as he'll ever be, I guess." Colin grabbed Sadie's arm to keep her from running into a street sign and smiled at her. "His cover story for Tobias is that the GWP thinks he's taking a private assignment for a friend but that he'll need to check in with them every few days so they don't think anything of his nefarious activities. He assured me that he would be in touch as often as he can. The GWP designed a device so he can send an SOS if he's in trouble."

Turning onto Cemetery Drive, we headed up the hill to the gated entrance then walked to the center of the cemetery, where the mausoleum was located, and went inside. Pops and Grams's tomb was located at the bottom, and Sadie and I sat in front of it, the guys sitting behind us.

Sadie couldn't hold back the tears when she saw that May 19, 2023, had been carved into the faceplate under Pops's name. All the times we'd come to visit Grams with him, that spot had been blank. I remember when Sadie and I were very little, I'd asked him why that part wasn't cut out, and he'd said because he wasn't ready to leave us yet; it would be many, many years before that happened. I ran my hand over the date, and Colin scooted closer to me and wrapped his arms around me.

"I miss him so much," I whispered. "Even though I didn't think he was my real grandfather, he always treated me like I was his granddaughter."

Sadie grabbed my hand and wiped the tear running down my cheek. "I can't imagine the thoughts that went through your head when you found out. We talked about it, but I know you didn't say everything."

I nodded and wiped the moisture from my other cheek. "Yeah, I was mad at first, but then, as time's gone by, I realized that he never treated us any different. I guess, from his side, he knew I was his granddaughter, so he didn't need to pretend."

I leaned back against Colin, and he squeezed me a little tighter. "I just wish I could remember if he taught us anything that calmed us down enough to clear our heads. I've tried thinking about the times we got hurt or something didn't go our way. He always comforted us, but he didn't give us any exercises or instructions." I looked away from the faceplate and over at Sadie. "Is the visit jogging anything in your memory?"

She shook her head and turned to face me a bit more before leaning against Luca again. "No. I just wish he'd made notes along the way that we could refer back to. The journals and diary were helpful, but not for this."

"You know, when we first met Raymond and he told us about what powers he thought you had, we found it hard to believe—especially when we found out your parents didn't have any paranormal abilities. He suspected that he would pass a few powers down to you, and it seems he was right. Knowing all this, I'm sure he instilled the knowledge in you somehow. You just need to figure out how." Colin squeezed me again. "Even if you do have certain powers, instinctively you'll use the stronger ones."

Sadie turned to Luca. "You've never told us what powers you two have."

"Our powers are a little more low-key than yours. We both have the power of the senses and power of clairaudience. We can hear when someone says our names from over five hundred miles away. When we became familiars, we acquired the power to sense when the person we are bound to needs help or is using their powers as well as the power of persuasion and power of amplification." Luca scooted around so he could lean against the stone near the faceplate.

"So, how exactly do your powers work?" I asked. "I thought you were just saying that the night you kissed me on the porch."

Luca grinned cheekily and shrugged. "Do you remember when we dropped off the first package from Raymond?"

I glanced at Sadie, and we smiled. "Oh, yes. We remember. Why do you ask?"

"Well, Raymond said that we needed to make you trust us. When we caught your eyes, we put the idea in your heads that we were trustworthy."

Colin peeked around to look at me, and my eyes went wide.

"So, our feelings were just you putting ideas in our heads?" I stared back at him.

He shook his head.

"Why did it seem like your gaze was magnetic, then?"

"Magnetic? How?" He furrowed his brow.

"When you turned to leave, it felt like I was being pulled. I had to catch myself." Sadie grabbed a strand of her hair and curled it around her finger.

Colin glanced at Luca and shrugged.

Luca smiled at Sadie. "Maybe it was because you thought we were cute."

It took me a couple of seconds to realize what he'd said, and I started choking on my spit.

Colin patted me on the back and leaned forward to meet my eyes. "I'm guessing from your reaction that Luca's right."

I shook my head and took a deep breath. "No." I peeked at Sadie lifting my brow, hoping she would help me out.

She smiled at me then turned to Luca. "We did think you were cute, but this feeling was much more powerful than that. Did you try to persuade us to do more than trust you?"

Luca glanced at Colin, and they both seemed speechless. Finally, they shook their heads.

"So, what does the power of amplification do?" I asked still watching them.

Colin cleared his throat. "We can loan you power. If you're performing a spell you're not strong enough to do alone, we can transfer our strength to you."

"Oh, so you're like a battery booster." I looked up at Colin.

Luca and Colin laughed, and they both seemed to relax a little. "Essentially, yes."

Sadie was giving Luca the side-eye.

"What's wrong, Sadie?" I asked.

She glanced at me then sat up to face Luca. "Is that why I could feel a pull while I was making that remedy?"

Luca nodded. "Yeah, I wanted to give you a taste of what it felt like. Is that bad?"

"No, it's not bad—I would just like to know beforehand."

Luca smiled. "Yes. But you knew about it when we were in the backyard doing the obstacle course for your ring spells. You need to learn to clear your mind before we can really do too much to help. Your power needs to flow freely first."

"That makes sense," Sadie said.

I gave a frustrated growl. "I just wish we could pick up on that like we've been able to with other abilities. Why didn't Pops leave us with meditation instructions if it's so important?"

"I mean, we could try asking him. I know we can't technically talk with the dead, but he did communicate through the herbs when we were talking about demons being unable to enter our world," Sadie pointed out.

I nodded. "And he did speak to me in my dreams while I was in the hospital," I recalled. "It's worth a shot." I turned back to the faceplate, placing my hand on their names as I closed my eyes. "Pops, Grams," I said as Sadie placed her hands on top of mine. "Can you please give us a sign or something to help us figure out how to relax enough to clear our minds? We're struggling right now and could really use your help."

I wasn't sure what I expected would happen, but after a minute with no visible attempt at communication from them, I stood and wiped off the back of my shorts. I blew Pops and Grams each a kiss and told them I loved them. Sadie did as well, and we turned to leave.

As we headed out of the mausoleum, I stopped, a sense of déjà vu sweeping over me. We were leaving on the day of Pops's funeral, when Sadie and I noticed two cats sitting on the sidewalk.

I turned to the guys. "I just realized you two were here for the funeral."

Colin kissed the top of my head and pulled me close. We walked across the cemetery and down toward Main Street. We hadn't eaten yet, so I called Carl's Pizza and placed an order for delivery. We arrived back at Roots & Remedies a few minutes later, and Neva and Cyrus updated us on the sales.

Ms. Ambrose came in at three thirty, just as I was helping Sadie finish bottling some tinctures in the kitchen.

As I caught sight of her approaching the counter, I gasped, dropping the bottle to rush out to the front room. "Oh, my goodness. Ms. Ambrose, what happened?"

She gave me a half smile as she rubbed her hand along the cast encasing her hand to halfway up her upper arm. "My ex found me two days ago. He's in jail right now, but the sheriff said they can only hold him a week unless the magistrate refuses him a bond."

"Did he do that too?" I asked, gesturing to her black eye and bruised cheek.

She nodded, reaching up to gently touch her cheek and flinching. "I'm looking for a place to stay where he can't find me. I'm scared that, next time, I might not be alive afterward."

"Is that the friend you're staying with?" I tilted my chin toward the lady standing near the front window.

"Yes. That's Nancy. She's scared to let me out of her sight."

"I can understand why." I paused, trying to think of something to say. "I finished your stone. You can pick out a chain for it." I placed the stone on a piece of black velvet on the counter near her. Dread filled me at the thought of her ex finding her again.

"*Charge a stone for her that will keep her hidden from him,*" Colin suggested telepathically from the kitchen.

"*Will you help me with it?*" I asked, worried I might not do it correctly.

"*Of course. Always, sunshine.*" I could hear his smile forming in his words.

"Ms. Ambrose. Do you have any other errands to run today?" I asked.

She looked up at me from the jewelry case. "I do. Nancy wants to teach me how to crochet. We need to go to Everything's Crafty to look at the yarn and needles. Why do you ask?" she asked, her brows furrowing.

I gave her a small smile. "I'd like to charge an extra stone for you. It shouldn't take me more than thirty minutes. Can you come back after you check out at the yarn?"

She nodded. "We can do that." Her gaze dropped to the jewelry case, and she pointed to the thicker sterling silver chain. "I'd like to get this one, please. I don't want a thin one. I'm afraid I'd break it."

"Yes, ma'am." I pulled out the chain and unhooked the clasp to slip the stone onto it. "Would you like to wear it now?" I asked, already knowing the answer.

"Yes, please."

Colin approached from the kitchen and extended his hand toward me. I handed him the pendant, and he met Ms. Ambrose's gaze.

"May I?" he asked, holding out the necklace.

She smiled. "That would be wonderful, young man. Thank you."

Stepping out from behind the counter, he stopped behind her and carefully lifted the necklace over her head. She moved her hair to the side so he could hook the clasp. "Is this length good for you? Does it sit okay?"

She reached up and placed her hand over the stone. "It's perfect. Thank you both so much. It's beautiful. How much do I owe you, my dear?"

I rang up the stone and the chain on the register. "It's $79.54 total."

Her eyes went wide, and she handed me a hundred-dollar bill. "Please keep the change. The peace of mind this will provide is worth way more than you're charging me."

I smiled. "I'm glad I could get it done for you. I should have your other stone charged shortly."

She nodded. "Thank you again."

I watched as she walked to the front door and Nancy opened it so it wouldn't hit her arm.

I turned to Colin. "What would be the best stone for this charge?"

He opened the jewelry case of pocket stones and pulled out a black tourmaline. "This is considered the king of protection. It forms a shield around the person carrying it."

I took a few minutes to think about how to phrase the intentions for the charge. "So, I would say I want the stone to put a protective shield around the carrier to keep them hidden. Right?"

He bit his bottom lip to stifle his smile. "That's right, sunshine. Now you just need to write it down to finalize the spell." He pulled me close and kissed me fast and hard before letting me go.

Heat rose in my cheeks as I sat carefully in my chair and grabbed my bag that hung on the back of it to get my journal and pen. Opening my journal, I started writing. A few minutes later, the letters glowed a bright reddish pink before going back to the black ink, activating the spell. I gripped the stone in my hand and lifted it to my chest, chanting the charging spell as I forced my intentions into the stone. The stone warmed in my hand, confirming my success, so I pulled out a velvet pouch for Ms. Ambrose to keep it in.

About fifteen minutes later, Ms. Ambrose and Nancy came back into the shop, carrying two bags of yarn.

"It looks like you'll be doing a lot of beautiful pieces with those pretty colors of yarn," I observed.

She smiled and looked at Nancy. "Yes. I hope I can catch on quickly. I should be able to practice with some of the basic stitches while I'm in my cast."

I pulled the purple velvet pouch from the box beside the register and set it on the counter. "That sounds wonderful." Opening the drawstrings, I took out the stone. "This will work alongside your necklace. It's black tourmaline and will form a protective shield to keep you hidden. If your ex comes looking for you, he won't be able to see or touch you until you touch him or say something to him directly."

Tears filled her eyes as she stared at the stone in my hand.

I held it out so she could take it. "He will never find you again unless you want him to."

She wiped the tears flowing from her eyes. "You don't know how much this means to me. How much do I owe you?"

I shook my head and smiled. "Not a thing. Consider it a gift. It gives me peace of mind knowing that you will be safe."

She walked around the edge of the counter. "Can I give you a hug?"

I handed the velvet pouch to Nancy and took a step to the right to stand in front of Ms. Ambrose. I carefully wrapped her in a hug, avoiding bumping her arm or cheek. "I would love to see you the next time you come to Salem. So I know you are safe." I took a step back.

"What is your name, my dear?" she asked, her eyes still full of tears.

I smiled. "Izzy."

She dabbed at the tear that snuck down her cheek. "Well, Izzy, I will definitely stop by. You are truly my guardian angel."

Heat filled my cheeks. "I'm glad you kept looking for the first stone. You are safe now."

She tightened her hand around the tourmaline, placed it in the pouch Nancy held open for her, then slipped it into her pocket. "I'll see you soon, Izzy." She leaned over to wave at Colin, who sat at the kitchen island before smiling at me. "Thank you again."

I gave her a quick nod. "You are very welcome, Ms. Ambrose."

"Please call me Mary."

"You are very welcome, Mary. Be safe going home."

Mary and Nancy waved before turning to leave the shop.

Once they were out the door, Colin came up beside me and kissed my cheek. "You did good, sunshine. I'm so proud of you."

I laid my head against his chest. "Thank you."

We joined Sadie and Luca in the kitchen again a couple of minutes later, and I filled them in on what had happened to Mary. "I guess your premonition about her was true. Thank you for pushing me to try carving it. I think the protection stone combined with the sigil will keep her safe, and the black tourmaline will keep her hidden."

She wiped her hands on the towel and wrapped me in a hug. "I knew you could do it."

We tried to relax and meditate when we got home, but we didn't feel any different than usual afterward. We decided to call it a night. I wasn't in the mood to try the CARDS technique for an answer in my dreams, so I lay tossing and turning for two hours before I finally fell asleep.

Chapter Nineteen

Tuesday, July 4, 2023

Sadie

Luca came in and woke me at eight fifteen, and I jumped out of bed to get ready to head to the shop. The guys turned into their cat forms and slept in the window all morning.

At around eleven, I slid my chair over to Izzy's desk. "I had a very odd dream last night about Pops and Grams," I said, keeping my voice low so Colin and Luca wouldn't hear me. Maybe I was being silly, but I wanted to run it by Izzy and test my theory before I got their hopes up.

Her eyes got big, and she turned toward me. "Did it have anything to do with how Pops would put us to bed at night?"

I slowly nodded. "Yes, the tea, the cool breeze from the fan, that song he would hum to us while tucking us in really tight before turning off the light and keeping the bedroom door cracked just a little so the hall night-light could shine in."

Izzy's eyes shone with glassy moisture. I grabbed her hand and glanced toward the windows to make sure the guys weren't listening.

"Do you think that was to help us relax?" She wiped a tear from her cheek.

"It's possible, but that wasn't all of my dream." I rubbed my forehead.

"Did Pops and Grams tell us a story about two girls once we were asleep?"

I nodded. "How did we have the same exact dream? Is this another power we need to learn?"

"Gosh, I hope not. We have enough on our plates." She looked toward the front windows as if considering whether to run it by Colin and Luca.

"Since we aren't sure if this is what will relax us, let's not say anything about it to the guys until we see if it works."

"Okay. Do you think the story is about what powers we have?"

I smiled and put my hand on her arm. "I'm not sure, but the story seemed pretty superhero-ish."

She laughed, and out of the corner of my eye, I saw the cats turn to watch us. I slid my chair back to my desk, and the guys finally turned away. Izzy and I helped quite a few customers throughout the day, and I received a few orders for remedies while Izzy got an order for a necklace, bracelet, and earring set. Our moods had both lifted, and it was hard not to smile when our eyes met.

———————— ❧ ————————

We stood in the kitchen getting everything packed up so we could leave for the day. Binx and Smokey were still asleep in the window.

"*Binx, are you ready to go home?*" I asked telepathically. I glanced at Izzy when he didn't respond then handed her my bag and walked into the front room. "Binx! Smokey! Are you two coming home with us, or are you staying here all night?"

As I reached the window where Binx slept, he still hadn't responded or even twitched.

"Ha ha. Very funny, you two." I leaned in to tap Binx's head. "Binx!"

I lifted his paw and let it drop, and he still didn't stir.

Izzy reached the window where Smokey lay. "Smokey, get up." She rubbed his head, trying to get a response from him. "Sadie, what the heck is going on?"

I picked Binx up and turned to her. "Give me my bag and grab Smokey. Something's wrong. We'll get James to take us to the GWP. Maybe they have a medical ward. I have no clue how to explain this to a veterinarian."

We walked out the kitchen door and greenhouse, locking up behind us.

James stood at the edge of the greenhouse facing the alleyway and turned when he heard the door latch. His eyes widened. "Are they okay? Why are you carrying them?"

I shook my head as the tears I was trying to hold back spilled down my cheek. "Something's not right. We can't wake them."

He opened the back door to his car and took our bags so we could climb in the back seat, still holding Binx and Smokey.

Sliding in behind the steering wheel, he put our bags on the passenger seat beside him. "I'm taking you to the GWP. The paranormal medic there can see what's wrong with them."

"Okay. Please hurry, James," Izzy begged, leaning down to kiss the top of Smokey's head.

"Yes, ma'am." He pulled out of the alley onto Chester Street. "Have they been acting any differently today? They seemed fine this morning when we got here."

I watched Binx. "No. I have no clue what's wrong." I wiped the tears from my cheeks and repositioned him in my arms so I could climb out when we got to the GWP.

James pulled around behind the GWP and put the car in park, then grabbed our bags as he jumped out to open the car door for us. We followed James through the back entrance and down a long dark corridor to a flight of stairs.

James gestured for us to go ahead of him. "It's the first door on the left when you get to the top of the stairs. I'm right behind you."

I pushed open the door, and we all stopped just inside. Four beds lined one wall of the room. A row of cabinets occupied the opposite wall.

A man in his early sixties, wearing black scrubs, stepped through the doorway across the room. "Come lay them on the bed, ladies. What happened?"

"They were acting normal all day. They changed forms when we got to the shop and went to lie down in the front window. They looked up at every customer who came in today. But when we were getting ready to leave the shop after we closed, this is how we found them." I glanced at the lady that came into the room.

The man followed my gaze. "Darcy, can you please tell Celeste to come up here right away?"

"Yes, Doctor." She hurried out the door we just came in through.

The doctor listened to both cats with his stethoscope and took their vitals. "They sound fine, and their vitals are normal. Did Luca or Colin order any takeout today?"

Izzy shook her head. "No. Come to think of it, I haven't seen them eat anything today."

I shook my head. "I haven't either. Do you know what's wrong with them?"

He cocked his eyebrow. "Not yet. It seems as if they are just asleep, but they're in a very deep sleep."

Celeste came into the room and stopped at the foot of the bed. "Mason, do you know what could have caused this?"

"No, I'm afraid I don't. I'll draw some blood and see if they accidentally ingested something problematic." He crossed the room to a cabinet and started pulling out supplies.

Darcy slid two chairs over to us so we could sit.

Celeste sat on the edge of the bed and ran her finger over Smokey's front paw. "He won't be happy when he wakes."

Izzy looked up at Celeste. "Why do you say that?"

She placed her hand on his paw and took a deep breath. "Mason will have to shave a spot in his fur to draw the blood."

A giggle escaped me, and I glanced at Izzy. Her bottom lip quivered, her eyes filling with tears. I leaned over and wrapped my arms around her.

"They'll be fine," I assured her. "It won't hurt them."

"I know. I just don't want him to be mad. He loves his fur." She laid her head on my shoulder and turned so she could still see them.

The doctor came back and shaved a small spot on each of their front paws, exposing a vein. Izzy leaned toward Smokey and rubbed his cheek. The doctor drew a small vial of blood from Binx and Smokey and disappeared through the door he entered from.

We sat quietly for a few minutes before Celeste got a text message.

"I need to go downstairs for a few minutes. Will you two be okay while I'm gone?" she asked.

We nodded, and she turned to leave. As she exited, I glanced to find James standing just inside the door with my bag on one shoulder and Izzy's on the other. I jumped up to approach him.

"You didn't have to hold these, James." I took the bags from him.

"It's okay, Miss Sadie. I don't mind." He glanced at Binx and Smokey. "I hope they're okay. Are you and Miss Izzy all right?"

I shrugged. "Yeah, for now."

He nodded. "I'll be right here if you need anything."

I smiled up at him. "Thank you."

Turning, I walked back to the bed and moved my chair closer to pick up Binx's left paw. As I rubbed my finger back and forth over his toes, I spotted a scar on his paw. I moved the fur aside so

I could get a better look. "Izzy, he has the same scar on his hand in his cat form as he does when he's human. I hope they wake up and are okay. I want Luca and Colin to get their revenge on Tobias for torturing them. I'm so glad Pops freed them."

Izzy leaned down, kissed Smokey's head, and picked up his paw. "Me too."

The doctor came back into the room twenty minutes later wearing a blank expression as he held a piece of paper. "According to their blood work, nothing is present that isn't supposed to be. I don't know what's wrong with them."

"I do," Celeste said as she came back into the room. She stopped at the foot of their bed and sighed heavily.

James slid a chair up behind her and gently touched her arm, letting her know she could sit.

"The message I received a bit ago was from a prison guard downstairs. He said Maggie wanted to talk to me."

Izzy and I straightened.

"What did she want?" I asked, a bad feeling coming over me.

She rubbed Smokey's head and glanced up at the doctor. "You won't find anything in their system because it was given to them over a week ago. Maggie said the potion she gave Colin and Luca wasn't a love potion. She just wanted them to think that's what it was, but Tobias brought her here to give them that potion and chant the spell today so the guys would be out of the way when he comes through the rift in five days."

I gasped and covered my mouth, tears filling my eyes again. "What did she give them?"

When I glanced at Izzy, she had tears rolling down her cheeks.

Celeste laid her hand on top of mine. "She said it was a sleeping potion."

I tilted my head and braced for the worst. "You don't seem relieved about that. Can you not reverse it?"

She turned her eyes to Binx and Smokey. "I'm afraid not. The spell she used is from their realm. Their magic doesn't work like ours."

Izzy scooped Smokey up into her arms. "What happens to them if it doesn't get reversed?"

"They continue sleeping, I would assume. We don't know much about this magic." She paused to study Binx. "I have a crew coming here later tonight to see if they can reverse the spell."

"I thought Luca brought back a spell book from their realm. Has anyone translated it?" I asked, trying to exhaust every option.

Celeste wiped the tear that snuck down her cheek. "No, I'm sorry, girls. I've had the best of the best look at that spell book, and none even know where to start. I sent Paxton to get information from Maggie. Right now, he's our best chance."

Izzy wiped her cheek. "Can we stay with them for a while?" She scratched Smokey's cheek.

The doctor nodded. "Of course. Stay as long as you want."

Celeste sniffled and stood. "I'm going to call in more paranormals to work on this. If you need anything, Darcy or James will get it for you."

I nodded and gently picked Binx up. "Thank you."

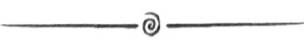

The town was having its big yearly fireworks show at nine, so we stood at the windows of the medical ward, holding Smokey and Binx as we watched them. We headed home an hour later. I'd never been so close to someone like this aside from Izzy. It had to be our bindings that made it feel like I was leaving most of my heart and soul with Binx when we left. I hated leaving them at the medical ward, but I had no clue how this spell worked, so it was best to let the doctor keep an eye on them.

Chapter Twenty
Wednesday, July 5, 2023

Izzy

As I hovered in the corner, listening to Tobias and one of his minions conversing, I felt sweat trickling down my brow. It had to be at least a hundred and ten degrees in his realm. Even though my body wasn't physically in his realm, I still felt its effects, and I knew Sadie would be trying to keep my body from overheating back at the shop.

Tobias slammed his fist on the table, snapping me out of my thoughts as I jumped.

"That rift is only open another eleven days, and it will take at least five more for my amulet to charge enough so my magic will work there. Once we get the spell book, I can reinforce the rift and transfer our energy into their power source to merge with ours, then our people can safely go through the rift before the lunar cycle is over. You just need to make sure our people are ready to go when the time comes. In fact, I want them ready before I leave in five days. My informant at their convent headquarters said those girls don't have powers, and since that old man is out of the picture, I won't have to worry about them fighting back. I can cast the spell that night."

Tobias dismissed his minion, then it was just me and him in the room. Though he couldn't see me, it still sent chills down my spine, and I shivered. Closing my eyes, I imagined I was back in Roots & Remedies with Sadie and not in this dreadful place.

I counted down from ten then slowly opened my eyes. Lying on the floor behind my desk, I could hear Sadie talking to a customer, so I grabbed the wet rag beside me and wiped the sweat from my face and neck. Thankfully, I could sense I was getting ready to blink because an intense hot flash gave me just enough notice that I could lie down before falling out of my chair and hurting myself.

Sadie noticed my subtle movements and glanced toward me, a small smile forming as she finished up with her customer. After they left, Sadie helped me back into my chair, and I filled her in on what I had seen and heard from Tobias.

During my vision, Sadie had sent Celeste a message that I was having another blink, and Celeste arrived about thirty minutes later to find out what I had learned. I filled her in on what Tobias had said, and she pondered the information a bit longer than normal.

Finally, she took our hands and sighed. "I'm going to get Neva to stay with you two while you're at the shop. I don't want you by yourselves with the guys under that spell. James and his team will be keeping watch outside the shop and your house until we get Tobias. As for the GWP member who is supplying Tobias with information, it sounds like a blackmail situation. I'll reassess our members and see if anyone stands out. Whoever it is must not want to hand over the information if they're giving Tobias bad intel."

Sadie's brow rose. "I hope Tobias isn't threatening to hurt the person."

I nodded. "But from what we know of the demon, that's probably the only thing he can threaten."

Celeste tilted her head. "We will do our best to find out who it is and get them and their family into protective custody until Tobias is captured. We're still working on the plan. At least we now know when he will arrive and that people are coming with him to the rift. Cyrus learned that their people can't see the GWP because of the glamours. We intend to take full advantage of that."

Sadie twirled a strand of her energy between her fingers. "Can we do anything about his powers?"

"Cyrus is trying to get information from Tobias about how his powers will work in our realm. I assume that his amulet will provide him with his power while he's here." She took a deep breath and exhaled slowly. "I just wish we had realized twenty-one years ago who we were dealing with. Lord Heldrum of the pixie realm is thankfully working with Tyson to figure out the signals we need to look for since their realm works like Demoria."

I gasped and looked at Sadie. "The pixie realm? I thought they lived in the forest behind Barnaby's shop."

Celeste giggled. "Yes, my dear. They do. A large rift there is always open to their realm. The way we believe the realms work is that Demoria would be a level below us, while the pixie realm is parallel to ours."

I huffed. "Well, if Demoria is under us, that makes sense. I can feel the heat from that realm when I blink. It's what I imagine hell would feel like. Plus, that's a good place for demons, since that's where evil beings are supposed to go when they die. Tobias fits in there well."

"Yes, he does. He deserves to live there even if his realm is dying," Sadie said.

Celeste glanced up from the necklace she was studying. "We don't believe his realm itself is dying. We think their magical power source is. Cyrus mentioned his world seemed perfectly fine aside from the heat difference. Their power source is kind of like ours under the GWP."

I shook my head. "I just wish we could close that rift and block him forever."

She nodded. "I do as well. That is also something we hope to figure out."

Chapter Twenty-One

Wednesday, July 5, 2023

Izzy

As I sat trying to ignore my growling stomach, something caught my eye on the edge of my desk. A green flicker of light reflected off it, and I stood to get a closer look. Leaning in, I noticed it wasn't green but black. A spider crawled along the edge. I carefully put my hand in front of her so I could take her outside to the greenhouse, where she could find food.

"What are you doing?" Sadie asked as I passed her in the kitchen.

"I found a spider. I'm gonna put her outside so she can find some food."

I walked to the spider plant that Pops had planted years ago and held the spider up to it so she could explore her new home.

As I closed the kitchen door, I stopped and faced Sadie. "I'm so glad Pops read *Charlotte's Web* to us when we were little. I never would have been brave enough to move them to another spot otherwise."

Sadie turned to me. "Did you make a wish as you released her?"

Pops had told us when he read us *Charlotte's Web* that if we moved a spider to a safe place, they would grant us one wish.

I reached down and found the cat charm on my bracelet that Colin got me not long after we met. "I did. I wished for the guys to wake up. Do you think they will anytime soon?"

She shrugged. "I'm not sure. I hope so."

I sighed. "I hope so too."

Neva came in through the kitchen door with the boneless wings and chef salads we ordered from Carl's Pizza. She placed the box on the counter, and I grabbed plates and napkins while Sadie got our drinks.

Swallowing a bite of chicken, I followed it with a sip of my soda. "Do you remember seeing *Charlotte's Web* on our bookshelf the other day?"

Sadie shook her head. "No. That book is on Grams's shelf. It was her favorite." Her brows furrowed. "Do you think that's the book we need to break the code?"

I shrugged. "I guess it can't hurt to check. I would have thought he'd use a book in his office since he didn't reference a specific one."

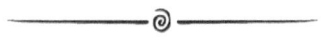

I went to the shelf in Pops's office that held all of Grams's favorite books and grabbed *Charlotte's Web*. The book was a lot thinner than I remembered as a kid. Then I sat at the dining room table and flipped to the first page of my notebook and waited for Sadie to finish putting our dinner in the oven.

She came and sat beside me and set a soda in front of me. "If this isn't the book, I don't know where else to look. None of the cookbooks worked."

I turned the paper over that held Pops's code. I figured we should start on the full page. As we flipped through the book's pages and scanned to the word then the letter, Sadie wrote it down, and we moved to the next combination in the code. At first, it didn't make sense, but as I translated it with the codex we made with Pops as kids, it started to decipher the book's code.

After about thirty minutes, we had finally deciphered the code Pops left us. *Salem Public Library the Discovery of Witchcraft Reginald Scot First Edition & New Edition* was written on the page of my notebook.

I looked at Sadie. "Well, I guess we need to go to the library."

Sadie nodded. "Yeah. We can close the shop for lunch tomorrow and go. They will be closed by the time dinner is ready."

"Agreed. And tonight we can work more on our elemental powers."

After forty-five minutes and zero success with our elemental powers, Sadie and I sat on the porch. Joey, the squirrel that lived in the tree in our backyard with his family, scurried down and stopped in front of Sadie. He squeaked at her, and she shook her head.

"They're in the medical ward. They were put under a sleeping spell," she said before she turned her attention to Joey's kids, Stumpy and Annie, who were playing in the strawberry patch at the base of the tree.

Sadie could hear Joey like I could hear Simba. Between the two of us, we could understand all animals. Joey could understand me, but I only heard squeaks when he replied. Sadie started filling Joey in on how the guys ended up being put under the spell, and I ran inside to get the bag of walnuts I had gotten for them from Barnaby's with our last order.

I sat back down on the porch and grabbed a handful of walnuts from the bag. I held my hand out to Joey, and he took one. Turning to his kids, he squeaked at them. They scurried out of the strawberry patch to sit beside Joey. I slowly extended my arm, offering them a walnut. Annie approached cautiously and sniffed my palm before taking a walnut with her mouth. Stumpy lifted his little nose into the air, and it started twitching. I pinched a single walnut with my thumb and first finger and lowered my hand so he could take it. He stood on his back legs and reached out with his front paws, carefully grabbing it. Then he stuffed the walnut piece into his mouth and reached for another one, resting his paw on the tip of my finger while grabbing one from the pile in my palm.

Stumpy scurried back up into the tree where his mom sat and set the walnut in front of her, then chewed the one in his mouth. She nuzzled him before he came back down the tree to get another piece. The kids went back and forth, getting walnuts and burying them in the strawberry patch and taking a few more up to their mom before the sun went down enough that Fergus, the garden gnome, woke and fussed at them for digging in the strawberries. They scurried back into the tree, Joey close behind.

Sadie went and grabbed a couple of crackers, slices of cheese, and a cookie. "Here ya go, Fergus. I hope you have a good night."

The gnome grunted at Sadie before grabbing the cookie and sitting on the edge of the porch. Sadie shook her head and walked inside.

I followed her and closed and locked the door. "He's not always that grumpy." I turned to look out at him. "Well, he wasn't grumpy when he woke me up that night the warlock was in our house."

"The gnome at Barnaby's was just as grumpy. Must be their nature," she said, watching Fergus.

"Have you noticed you've either woken them up or are interacting with them as soon as they wake up? That could be why they're grumpy. They haven't had their version of morning coffee yet," I suggested.

"Yeah, I guess that makes sense. Maybe I'll catch him in a good mood one of these days." She let out a big yawn and rubbed her eyes. "I'm gonna go to bed. It's been a long day, and I'm not sleeping that well without the guys here."

I nodded. "Me either. I'm right behind you." I turned off the light in the dining room and pulled the curtain closed over the sliding glass door and followed Sadie down the hallway to our rooms. I did our nighttime routine and tried calling on my dreams to figure out how to wake Colin and Luca. We had to have some kind of good luck soon.

Chapter Twenty-Two

Thursday, July 6, 2023

Sadie

Nothing had changed for the guys when we arrived this morning. Our attempts at feeling our elemental powers had been a pure failure the previous night as well. We were starting to feel like Tobias had already defeated us. The only thing we had going for us was that we actually had no clue where Hazel's spell book was.

As I rubbed Binx's head, Celeste came in and sat beside me on his bed.

"Have you had any luck with your elemental powers yet?" She reached over and rubbed his paw.

I wiped the tear that fell from my eye. "No. I thought the earth elemental power would be easy since we can both draw our power from the earth, but we aren't having any luck. I can get a strand of ivy to slowly wrap itself around my finger when I put it close, but I can't get it to do anything else."

Celeste smiled. "The power you pull from the earth is much different from your earth elemental power. The elemental side allows you to control things such as vines, plants, animals, metals, and stones." She looked at Izzy. "Izzy will probably be able to control metals and stones sooner than vines and plants."

Izzy picked up Smokey and came to sit on the bed with us. "Is that because I have more of a connection with them since I work with them?"

Celeste scratched the top of Smokey's head. "It is. Because you already have a strong connection with them, they should recognize when you call to them. If you have one sitting in the center of your desk, don't move toward it. Let it come to you." She turned her attention back to me. "The same goes for the plants and ivy. Let the plants come to you. Remember they are living and you don't want to scare them off. You want them to trust you."

I huffed. "That sounds so odd to me. I never thought a plant or stones could trust people."

She nodded and giggled. "When I was young, I used to love throwing stones and pulling the leaves off the trees for no reason other than I was bored. My father sat me down and explained that same thing to me. I thought he was crazy until I came into my powers and went to meet Aztec."

Izzy gasped at the mention of the elder raccoon who, along with his mate, Queenie, had helped us once before. "Did Aztec help you feel your powers too?"

She nodded and looked down at her black onyx ring. "He did. Queenie helped me with my breathing techniques and meditation. Growing up, I didn't want to follow in my father's footsteps. I'd lost my mother when I was very young, and I rebelled every chance

I got. Then, when my father took me to the realm where the pixies live, my attitude toward my magic completely changed."

"Did your father help you learn your powers?"

She chuckled and leaned back against the bed's footboard. "No. I still rebelled against him, but the critters in the pixie realm were more than helpful in my training."

Izzy nodded and smiled as she stroked Smokey's thick fur. "If it hadn't been for Aztec sharing his essence with me, I don't know that I ever would have felt my energy."

Celeste sat back up. "I'd like to send someone to help you with your elemental powers who I think you will relate to a little more than Felix. Marissa Turner came to Salem as a child. She had been picked on when she was younger because of things that happened randomly with her powers. She ended up running away at the age of fourteen, when she was found by a member of the GWP and brought to us. Marissa was not born a green or celestial witch, and from what we learned later on, she had four of the five elemental powers. We contacted her parents, and they allowed us to teach her to control her powers. They were thankfully very understanding and wanted the best for Marissa."

I looked up from Binx with my brows furrowed. "Does she own Enchanted Scoops? Pops took us there when we were little. I used to call her Rissa 'cause I couldn't say Marissa."

Celeste nodded. "Yes. She does. Her specialty is working with cryokinesis. She wanted to have a business where she could use her powers. Her favorites were always water and air."

Izzy smiled from ear to ear. "That's very clever. I'd love to work with her."

I nodded.

Celeste stood with a grin. "I'll get in touch with her and see when she can meet with you. You can use the arena again. I'll let you two get back to your visit with Binx and Smokey, and I'll message you once I set a time."

Izzy and I both thanked Celeste, and she gave a petite curtsy and turned to leave.

Maybe Marissa could give a bit more insight about the feelings or emotions we should be having while learning the elemental powers. Luca, Colin, and Felix meant well, but men weren't normally as sensitive to that type of thing. I still wished Binx and Smokey were awake. It had been so hard to focus the past few days without them.

Chapter Twenty-Three

Thursday, July 6, 2023

Izzy

I got a message from Celeste just before lunch asking if we could meet Marissa at the arena at six after we closed. I asked Sadie if that worked for her, and she agreed.

We closed the shop for lunch and went to the Salem library. The librarian said she could let us look at the first edition but, due to its age and value, it had to stay there. She brought the book out from the archives room and set two pairs of gloves on top of it. We carried it to the table, and Sadie went to look for the new edition.

I slipped on my gloves and started carefully flipping through the book, looking for marks or anything that Pops could have left us. About a third of the way through the book, I found a folded piece of paper, the same type of paper that Pops always used.

Sadie sat beside me. "Someone has the new edition checked out right now, but it's due back in two days. What's that?" She pointed to the paper folded between the pages.

"I'm not sure." I removed it carefully and opened it.

Inside was another code like the one we had to decode from *Charlotte's Web*. "I guess Pops hid the code in this one, and we'll need the new edition to decipher this code. What is with Pops and his puzzles?"

Sadie shrugged. "I guess he thought he needed several layers of security to keep the book safe. We can come back to get the new edition after Tobias is captured. I don't want to risk him being able to read our minds and finding the location if this code holds the answer."

I nodded. "Good point." I closed the book carefully and carried it back to the librarian, then slipped the gloves off and laid them beside the book.

We thanked her and left to go back to the shop to finish out the day.

We closed at five thirty since the shop hadn't been busy. Sadie had spent most of the day restocking the shelves while I worked on a few more obsidian stone carvings. I was finally catching on to where the stones would cause problems and make the Dremel kick.

We decided to walk to the arena since it was a somewhat nice day. The past three days had been in the nineties, and currently, it was in the low eighties, so it was much more tolerable outside. James even decided to walk with us.

We arrived at the arena and gathered the items from the shed to set up the courses. A couple of minutes before six, Celeste and Marissa came down through the bleachers and onto the field.

Celeste did our official introductions as GWP members, though we'd met years ago.

Marissa looked around at the courses and smiled. "You guys must have had training recently. This is exactly what I would have set up."

Sadie grinned as she placed the candles on the log. "Did you work with Felix, too, when you were learning how to control your powers?"

Marissa lowered her head as she turned her ring on her finger. "I did. He was stationed here in Salem when I arrived. He was the one who discovered I wasn't actually born a witch. I had just developed the power to control the four elements."

I watched her as she continued twisting her ring. "If you don't mind me asking, which one can you not control?"

She met my eyes. "I can't control the spirit element. It took me two years of training and learning about the elements before I could wield any of them correctly."

"I know this is probably a sensitive subject, and you don't have to tell us anything if you don't feel comfortable."

She smiled. "That was when I was younger because I didn't know what was going on. But ask away. I wanna help as much as I can. I know what you two are up against. I couldn't imagine the pressure you must feel."

I shrugged. "I just wish we started training at a young age. It's a bit overwhelming to learn everything all at once—especially with the guys in the medical ward upstairs." I took a deep breath. "Celeste mentioned you ran away from home because of your powers. What types of things were happening?"

She leaned against the large hay bale that we had blasted with energy balls a few weeks back. "I'm from Madison County. The small private school I went to was in an old building. In the main room where we learned most of our subjects was a huge fireplace. Anytime I walked near it, the flames would grow a lot bigger, and a spark would jump out at me. It started fires twice before I stayed on the opposite side of the room from it. I got in trouble both times, and the principal even threatened to kick me out if I threw anything else into the fire.

"When I went to wash my hands in the bathroom, the water would turn on full blast and splash all over the floor and down the front of me. When the weather was nice and we had the windows open, anytime I caught people staring at me, a big gust of wind would come through the window and blow their papers off their desk.

"I was a loner for so long because of all that and was always more comfortable in the garden in the back of the school. I loved sitting with the ivy plant. It was so nice when the vines would wrap themselves around my wrists. One of the teachers caught me outside with my hand out and the vines coming to me as I spoke to them, and it freaked her out so bad that she told the principal that if he didn't expel me, she would quit. So he did.

"My parents were always on my side, but they didn't know what was causing it. The day after I was expelled, I packed a bag and the journal I had been keeping and left home to figure out what was wrong with me. I mailed postcards to my parents once a week from random places to let them know I was okay. They would add money to my bank account every week for food. After about four months, I met someone from the GWP when I was at a restaurant in Shawsville. He said he could sense my power and could tell I needed help."

Sadie walked over to her and gave her a big hug. "I'm so sorry you had to go through all that by yourself. Who found you? I want to thank them."

She smiled and grabbed the amethyst stone that hung around her neck. "It was Raymond."

I gasped. "Our grandfather Raymond?"

She nodded. "He had stopped to grab a bite to eat after going to Barnaby's."

I wiped the tear that had snuck down my cheek. "Is that why you agreed to help us? Because he helped you?"

Marissa shrugged. "I would have helped you either way, but I've always felt that I owed Raymond, and he never let me pay him back in any way. You might not remember this, but at the Halloween festival when you two were little, you were sitting and watching the parade, and I brought you both a cone of your favorite ice cream, and I wouldn't let Raymond pay me for it. The next morning when I came to open the store, an envelope with twenty dollars was taped to the door. Someone had written 'Nice Try' on the front. He told me the next time he came in that I didn't owe him anything."

I chuckled. "That sounds like Pops. He used to tell us our money was no good if he was around."

Sadie sniffled and wiped her eyes. "Did Pops give you that necklace?"

She nodded and held it out so we could see it. "He gave it to me the day I graduated from my training. He said it brought out the color of my eyes. I haven't taken it off since." She wrapped her hand around the stone and tucked it back into her shirt. "Well, that's enough about me. Tell me about your journey so I know where I can start to help."

Sadie and I both wiped our eyes again. I pointed to the bleachers, and Sadie and Marissa headed over to sit down. With Marissa between us, we started filling her in on how we found out about our powers and what we knew had happened with them when we were younger—the candle flame growing at Sadie's birthday party when she was thirteen and when I felt like I was floating when I fell off my top bunk that same year.

"Have you been able to find your calm?" Marissa asked as she looked from Sadie to me.

Sadie's brows furrowed. "Find our calm?"

She nodded. "Yes, with your relaxation and meditation."

"Oh, that. I think we have, but the guys were put under that spell after we figured it out, so we haven't had a chance to test it, but we've been doing the techniques every night since then."

"Okay, that's wonderful. Have you been able to make anything happen with the elements?" she asked as she stood up.

"I managed to make a stone move about an inch toward me earlier today, and Sadie got the ivy in the shop to come to her instead of her going to it. But that's all so far."

Marissa shook her head and waved her hand for us to follow her. We stopped at the course where we would work on the fire elemental power. As Marissa explained what to do, that dreadful breeze swept through the arena. I knew another one was coming because it always seemed to come back around. The air got a tad colder, and I reached up and swirled my hand in the air as if to catch cotton candy as it was being made. Once the air warmed slightly, I slammed my fists toward the ground, creating a large dent in the grass. Sadie and Marissa stood staring at me in shock.

Sadie blinked a couple of times at the ground then back at me. "What in the hell was that?"

I stared at my hands then looked down at the grass. "Every time we're here, this cold breeze comes through, and it covers me in goose bumps. I don't know how or why, but I wanted it to stop, so I grabbed it."

Sadie shook her head as she processed my words. "How did you know it would work?"

"Every time it sweeps in, I feel like I can see it. It reminds me of a picture that was in the art museum where the artist had painted a windy fall day. I just imagined I could grab it, and I could." I met Sadie's eyes. "You don't feel that cold breeze here?"

I glanced at Marissa, and she was smiling.

"That's the trick to these elements. It's the air on our skin, the heat of the fire, the moisture of the water, and the texture of the earth. These powers aren't something you feel inside you like when you draw power from the earth."

Marissa agreed to work with us for the next three days. She gave us a few things to start with that helped her and said, by the end of the weekend, she hoped to have us throwing air, fire, and water balls. We took notes on our phones like the guys had done that day with Felix, and we thanked Marissa and started cleaning up so we could head home and get to work. We just had one pit stop to make before going home.

We told Binx and Smokey about working with Marissa and promised them that we would get their spell removed as soon as we could. It was the first time Sadie and I left the GWP medical ward feeling like things would actually be okay.

Chapter Twenty-Four

Friday, July 7, 2023

Sadie

I woke early this morning from a very intense dream. I had found an ancient spell book containing a spell for a demonized sleeping potion, and when I told Izzy about it at breakfast, she insisted we visit Kitty Parker at Parchment & Scratch.

"Sadie, you know our dreams always have reasons behind them. We need to look into it more." She shoved the box of granola bars in her bag that had been delivered with our grocery order the night before.

"Yeah, I know. I just hope we can find the right one. I didn't see the book's cover." I let out a heavy sigh. "Well, since I couldn't go back to sleep this morning, I worked on my earth elemental power. When I put my hand out to the ivy plant, I imagined that I was touching the fuzzy strands of the vine, and the vine came down and wrapped around my finger. When I started rubbing the vine, it seemed like that specific strand relaxed. As I raised another finger, it wound itself farther around my first finger to reach the other one. It kinda reminded me of when a cat leans into your hand when you're petting it."

Izzy smiled. "That's so neat. I couldn't fall asleep last night and was lying in bed with a jasper stone that I hadn't charged or anything yet, and I tried calling it to me. I got it to slide across my nightstand to me, but it was much harder to get it to go across my comforter. I just kept imagining the smoothness of the stone and what the small imperfections felt like, and it started moving. I picked it up and moved it back after it came to me the first time, and when I tried to move it again, it didn't budge. I picked it up and rubbed it for a moment then laid it down again, and it came right to me. I guess what Celeste said about them being alive is true. I fell asleep rubbing the stone. It was still in my hand when I woke up."

I giggled. "Sounds like the stone wanted to be told it did a good job before it did it again. Maybe we can use that. Reward the flame if we get it to cooperate. Same with the earth, water, and air. Train it like you would a living animal."

Izzy's eyebrows rose, and she smiled. "I guess it can't hurt to try."

I looked at my watch for the time and jumped up. "Neva should be here any minute."

She had been going to the shop with us every day since the guys fell under that spell. She had been a huge help taking care of the customers and keeping us on track with making remedies and stuff for the shop. It was hard to tell how much we would have been moping around if she weren't there with us.

We arrived at the shop twenty minutes before we had to open. Neva told us to go get what we needed from Kitty, and she would prep the shop for us.

When we walked into the bookstore, Parchment & Scratch, Kitty was sitting behind the register. She smiled up at us and grabbed three books from under the register. "I had a feeling you two would be here to ask about these this morning."

I grinned. "How did you know that we would want these?"

She pointed to her head. "I had a dream about it. I also wrote down two books that Raymond bought from me that may help you as well. The paper's inside the top book."

I ran my hand across the book's cover. "How much do we owe you?"

She shook her head. "Not a thing, girls. You just wake those two boys up soon. I hate knowing they're under that spell."

Izzy smiled. "We'll do our best, Kitty. Thank you so much."

I nodded. "Yes. We appreciate it more than you know."

She shooed us off with her hands. Sadie and I giggled and waved as we left.

Back at Roots & Remedies, we showed the books to Neva, and she offered to look through the third book for anything that would help. I went to the kitchen so Neva could use my desk and help customers as they came in. Izzy got to work flipping through her book, marking pages she thought we could use at some time or another. I riffled through my book as I waited for the cocoa butter to melt in the double boiler. I had made it about halfway through my book when Izzy and Neva came into the kitchen.

Neva opened her book to a page she had marked. "What do you think of this one? The spells in this book seem to make something evil happen or reverse something evil. This one is supposed to reverse a sleeping potion."

Izzy took over stirring the cocoa butter so I could look more closely at the recipe. "I don't know if this is the right one, but I definitely want to try it. I have everything here except mugwort. I'd like to close for an hour at lunch so we can run to the house to get the mugwort and go to the medical ward to see if it works. I don't wanna wait until we close."

Izzy nodded and grabbed her phone to update the shop's social media pages about closing for lunch. Neva made a sign for the front door and taped it up. I got to work mixing the recipe. I made four doses just in case one wasn't strong enough. If this doesn't work, we would need to figure out something else. I missed Luca, and I knew Izzy missed Colin.

The morning seemed to drag by so slowly after I made the potions. James came inside the shop at five minutes to noon and offered to drive us since we only planned to be closed for an hour.

We locked up the shop, went by the house to get the mugwort, and added it, then we were off the see Binx and Smokey.

I asked Darcy if she could send the doctor to monitor the guys while Izzy and I gave them the potions in case they had a bad reaction. Using a syringe, we gave them the first dose and watched for about five minutes before giving them the second one. A minute later, they moved their paws a couple of times, but that was all. The potion wasn't strong enough. I asked the doctor if I should mix a couple more, but he warned against it because the amount of mugwort in it could cause kidney damage or worse.

Izzy wiped her tears, and she kissed the top of Smokey's head.

I leaned down and kissed Binx on his cheek. "I'm so sorry that didn't work. Back to the drawing board. I wish you were here with me at least telepathically to help figure this out."

Izzy and I decided to walk back to the shop, and James followed close behind.

As we walked, Izzy let out a heavy sigh. "Did Luca promise you that he would be with you for every step of our training and when we go up against Tobias?"

I nodded. "Not in those exact words, but yes."

"I want to be mad at Colin for going back on his word, but how could he have ever known something like this would happen?" she asked as we turned the corner onto Main Street. "I feel so bad that we sort of forced them to have dinner with Maggie and Beth."

I grabbed her hand. "We can't really hold them responsible for this, or us for the matter. None of us knew anything about this spell work."

She tapped the top of my hand. "Yeah. I guess you're right. I just miss them both so much."

My breath hitched at her comment. "Me too."

Chapter Twenty-Five

Saturday, July 8, 2023

Sadie

When I woke, I had a message from Neva saying that Mel would be spending the morning at the shop with us, but she didn't mention why. Mel was waiting at the back of the shop, looking in the greenhouse window. She smiled when she saw us coming up the alley and went to stand at the door.

As we got closer, she pointed to the window. "Looks like that spider has made itself at home in that spider plant."

Izzy smiled. "Oh, that's Charlotte. I moved her in there from my desk a few days ago. She's made a beautiful web."

Mel glanced back toward the window. "She needs to find herself a Wilbur and have some babies. That was my favorite book as a child."

I nodded. "Pops read it to us when we were younger. It was Grams's favorite book too."

"I loved hearing stories about her. She was an amazing person."

I unlocked the door to the greenhouse, and we went inside with Izzy locking the door behind us. We all put our stuff down on the island.

I looked at Mel. "Is Neva okay? I had a text from her when I woke up, but she didn't say why she wouldn't be here."

"Oh yes. She's fine. She got a message from Cyrus. He sent a raven back through the rift last night, so she's at the GWP helping them come up with a plan. She asked me if I could come stay with you for a while."

Izzy grabbed us all a bottle of water. "Did she say what was in his note?"

"She said they needed to find out how to close the rift. Apparently, once Tobias comes through it, his amulet will stay attached to his world. If we can close the rift, his powers won't work." Mel took a sip of water. "I think they're trying to write a spell to close it for good. If Tobias puts Cyrus under a spell before he returns, once we close the rift, the spell will be broken."

My brows shot up. "That would definitely work to our advantage. I hope they can come up with something."

Mel and Izzy both nodded. "Me too," they said at the same time.

Chapter Twenty-Six
Saturday, July 8, 2023

Izzy

Sitting at my desk, I tried to write a new charging spell, but I struggled to focus. We had seen results with our elemental powers. I had finally been able to throw a baseball-sized rock across the arena without touching it and could control my air power and manipulate the wind a lot more.

Sadie had put some birthday candles in her doughnut Mel had brought us this morning, and she could make the flames jump from one candle to the next. She could also make the water slosh around or splash from ten feet away and was making great strides with her earth element, which didn't surprise me, since she had been so close to plants from a young age.

Marissa had helped us realize how to manipulate our elemental powers very quickly. We still needed a lot of practice to strengthen them, but she said that would come in time. As long as I had a breeze of some kind and stone or metal close by, I should be okay defending myself.

I slid my journal closer to me and opened it to the binding spell Pops had written. I took a deep breath and slowly released it as I ran my fingers over the writing. As I reached the instructions part of the spell, a glowing green *S* appeared just above my fingers. I gasped as the letter *P* appeared right next to it. "Um. Sadie, something's happening."

Sadie and Mel ran into the front room, stopping on either side of me. I pointed at *spel* written along the page.

I looked up at Sadie. "I think its Pops trying to tell us something again."

We all waited and watched as the message appeared. *Spell book Luca grabbed.*

Mel's brows flew up. "What does he want you to do with the spell book?"

I shrugged. "Pops? What do you want us to do with it?"

A couple seconds later, the letter *G* appeared, and we waited for him to complete the message. *Go to it* was written just below where the first part of the message started to fade.

I tapped the screen on my phone for the time. It was a quarter to noon. I glanced at Sadie. "We can close for lunch and go tell Celeste that Pops wants us to look at it."

"Do you think we'll be able to read it?" Sadie asked as she finished tying the string on the lavender.

"I doubt it. I don't remember Pops ever teaching us anything with other languages." I pulled out the Closed for Lunch sign to hang it on the front door.

"Me either."

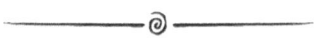

We arrived at the GWP a few minutes after twelve and waited in the basement with Tyson while Celeste went to get the spell book out of the warded lockbox in the storage room. I looked around the dark room where Tyson watched dozens of computers every day. I turned to him as he sipped a deep-red liquid through a straw.

"How do you deal with being down here without sunlight?"

Mel giggled. "I guess the guys never told you."

My brows furrowed. "Never told me what?"

Tyson stood and removed the lid from his cup. "What did you think I was drinking? It's not tomato juice."

Sadie peered into the cup. "Eww. What is it, then?"

Tyson stared at her with a confused expression. "Well, blood of course."

Sadie's eye widened, and she took a giant step back toward me, about five feet from him.

I looped my arm with Sadie's. "If you're drinking blood and staying in a dark basement, I'm going to assume that you're a vampire."

Sadie's body tensed as she waited for his reply.

He looked from me to Sadie. "Don't worry, ladies. This is animal blood. I have never fed off a human before, so you're safe."

Sadie's brows rose. "If you are a vampire, how are you still around and working for the GWP?"

Tyson leaned back in his chair and put his feet up on the desk. "My mother was nine months pregnant with me when she was bitten. She survived three days before she passed away giving birth to me. I was born at a covenant in Scotland, and the doctor who delivered me raised me as his own. Instead of drinking milk as a baby, I was given animal blood. As I grew up, I never had cravings for human blood. I eat all the same food humans eat, but the meat I consume is raw, and I drink blood instead of other liquids."

Sadie let out the breath she was holding. "After everything that's happened these last few months, I don't know how anything can still surprise me, but I thought vampires were a myth."

Tyson shook his head. "No. We are very much real. There aren't many of us left though. You will come to realize very soon that most things that go bump in the night, are very much real."

Celeste came into the room holding a large item wrapped in black velvet cloth. She set it on the empty table near the door and gently unwrapped it, revealing a very old book with writing on the front that I couldn't read. Sadie reached out to rub her hand over the cover as Tyson and Mel came up behind us.

Mel stepped a little closer and glanced at Celeste. "Demorian Grimoire?"

Celeste nodded. "That's what we assume it is."

Mel gazed at the book and ran her fingers along the foreign symbols. "Demorian Grimoire. That's what it says."

All eyes turned to Mel, and Tyson stepped a bit closer, his eyes shifting between the book and her. "You can read that?"

Mel's brows furrowed. "You can't?"

Tyson shook his head. "No. I have been staring at this book since Luca brought it back to this realm. I've had dozens of scholars and witches come look at it to decipher the writing with zero success. How can you read it?"

Mel carefully opened the cover to the first page and started reading off a list of ingredients. "It looks like it's written in our language."

Tyson's eyes widened as he met Celeste's gaze. "How is this possible?"

Celeste's expression shifted from shocked to elated. "We think she may have backed into the rift when she was in the alley where Donald found her unconscious. I assume some of their power transferred into her."

Mel jerked her head toward Celeste. "How much of it?"

Celeste shrugged. "I'm not sure."

I approached the table and slid the book closer to Mel. "Can you flip through and look for a spell to wake Binx and Smokey?"

She wrapped me in a hug. "I'll do anything I can to help."

Celeste shared a look with Tyson. "If she finds the correct spell to reverse this, I'll make the potion. Mel, will you stay and read this out loud so Tyson can type it into the system?"

Mel smiled and stood straighter. "I'd be happy to." She carefully picked up the book and turned to Tyson. "You might want to refill your animal juice. We'll be here awhile."

Mel and Tyson walked to his computer to get started, and I looked at Celeste.

"I guess Pops knew she could read it," I said.

Celeste grinned. "He always has been one step ahead."

We headed back to Roots & Remedies with the promise that they would call us as soon as she found something. James drove us back to the shop, and we entered with a lot more pep than when we left.

Chapter Twenty-Seven

Saturday, July 8, 2023

Sadie

Celeste sent us a message at half past three.

She did it. She found a spell that should wake Binx and Smokey. The recipe is very detailed and will take a couple of hours to make. I should hopefully have it ready by the time you close the shop, so come here straight after. We want you to be here when they wake up.

Izzy peeked into the kitchen. "Do you think it will work?"

I shrugged. "I'm not sure, but I really hope it does. I miss them."

The next hour and a half seemed to go by at a snail's speed. We decided to close at five since we hadn't had a single customer since we opened the shop that afternoon.

As we exited through the greenhouse door, I closed it tightly and turned toward Izzy when I suddenly got very dizzy. I closed my eyes to steady myself, and a vivid, colorful image flashed through my mind. I gasped and grabbed the wall of the greenhouse to keep from falling. After Izzy grabbed my arm, I was able to open my eyes.

She looked at me with concern. "What did you see?"

James approached to help me to the car, where I could sit with my feet still on the ground.

I took a deep breath and slowly released it. "We were sitting at the park on a blanket, and we were flipping through an old book, trying spells. In the distance, I caught a glimpse of Tobias watching us."

Izzy squatted in front of me. "What other details do you remember? Was anything on the blanket with us?"

I closed my eyes again, trying to search my image. "There was a picnic basket, a piece of black velvet, and..." I gasped. "The box that Celeste gave us that night after the meeting. The one that she wanted everyone to think held Hazel's spell book. I think this is what we'll be doing when Tobias arrives."

Izzy sighed heavily. "So, you see us pretending that the spell book is the real one to trick Tobias into thinking it's the one he wants?"

I rubbed my eyes and nodded. "As much as I don't like it, it might just work. He can't see our glamours, according to Cyrus, so we can have other paranormals hiding around us, waiting for him to make a move."

James gestured for me to get into the car all the way. "We need to get to the GWP to inform Celeste. I know they're putting together a plan. This idea might work better."

We found Celeste in the apothecary room, waiting for the potion to finish steeping into the vials. She looked up at us as we stepped inside.

"It's almost ready," she confirmed. "I really hope it works."

Izzy and I were silent, and Celeste frowned. "Did something happen, ladies? You look like something's on your mind."

Izzy and I nodded, and she stepped a bit closer.

"Sadie had another premonition," Izzy said.

Celeste put a cork in the vial she held and gave Izzy her full attention. "What did she see?"

Izzy told her about the scene, and it looked like she was trying to picture it.

"Do you think you would be okay putting yourselves in that situation?" she asked as she removed the second vial from the steeper and corked it.

Izzy glanced at me, and I nod. "Yeah. As long as we have reinforcements behind the glamours."

She gives us a curt nod and held up the vials. "Let's go see if we can wake the boys, and we can work out the details afterward."

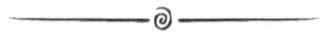

Darcy told the doctor that we had arrived, and he came out of his office to keep an eye on Smokey and Binx in case things went wrong.

Celeste tilted their heads to the side one at a time and slowly let the warm potion drip into their mouths. "This might take a minute." She set the vials aside and watched them.

As the seconds ticked by, it seemed as if it wasn't going to work. Then, suddenly, Binx spread his paw wide and started stretching as he yawned. My heartbeat sped up as I looked at Smokey, waiting for a sign that he might wake up. The doctor listened to his heart and lungs as Binx perked up a little more, then Smokey suddenly stretched and rolled onto his back. Izzy gasped.

Tears streamed down my cheeks as Binx looked at me through slitted eyes and yawned again.

"*Why are you crying?*" he asked me telepathically.

"*You don't realize where you are?*" I reached out and put my hand on his paw.

He stared at me for another moment before slowly looking around the room. About ten seconds later, his head jerked back toward me. "*Why am I in the medical ward?*"

I turned toward Izzy, who had Smokey in her arms as the doctor checked his vitals.

He nodded and sat in the chair beside the bed. I turned toward Celeste, but she had left the room.

Izzy huffed, and I turned to see Smokey trying to get out of her arms. He jumped down onto the bed beside Binx, and green and blue misty clouds formed around them. Izzy wiped her eyes as she waited for the clouds to dissipate, then she lunged at Colin, wrapping her arms around him.

Luca sat across from me with his back toward me. He looked down at his hands and slowly turned to face me. He reached up and wiped the tears from my cheeks. "What happened?"

"What's the last thing you two remember?" I glanced between them.

Luca and Colin closed their eyes as they tried to recall their last memories.

Luca tilted his head with one eye still closed. "We were sitting in the window at the shop."

Colin peered at Luca. "Yeah. That's the last thing I remember too. Why are we here?"

"Maggie and Beth put you under a sleeping spell," Celeste said from the doorway.

Luca and Colin shot each other a confused look.

Then Colin returned his attention to Celeste. "How did they do that? They've been in custody since the night they were arrested. Right?"

Celeste nodded. "Yeah. They slipped you the potion that night at dinner."

Luca's eyes widened. "I thought Maggie slipped something into our drinks but didn't feel any side effects. The potion should have been out of our system the next day."

She shook her head and walked to the foot of the bed. "It was a spell from their realm. They stay in your system a lot longer than ours do."

Colin's brows furrowed. "How did you reverse the spell?"

Izzy placed her hand on his arm. "Demorian magic."

Colin shook his head as if trying to clear the confusion filling it. "Okay. Start at the beginning, and don't leave anything out."

As we waited for the blood work to come back, Izzy and I filled them in on everything they had missed over the last few days, and we answered all their questions along the way.

The doctor gave them the all clear and told them he wanted to check on them again in a week. Now that the book Luca got from Demoria was being translated, he would hopefully know what to look for with future testing. I just hoped the power didn't have a negative effect on Mel.

Chapter Twenty-Eight

Saturday, July 8, 2023

Sadie

Tyson appeared in the medical ward just as we were about to leave. He smiled when he saw that Luca and Colin were awake. "It's nice to have you two back." He approached Celeste and handed her something.

She turned and smiled. "I couldn't sleep last night, and I was reminiscing about Raymond and all the assignments we went on together when I was younger." She held out a small blue velvet box. "I had forgotten all about these. I was with Raymond and his team when we went looking for them. My father, Atticus, sent for paranormals from all over the world to figure out what these did. Everyone who came said they could feel their power, but it did nothing to enhance their abilities. Go ahead and open it."

The box was about the size a bracelet would come in. I took it and carefully removed the lid. Inside were five separate compartments with cloth in each. I glanced at Izzy then back at the box before handing it to Izzy to hold as I pulled out the first piece of cloth. I carefully unwrapped what was inside, and Izzy and I gasped. Inside was a raindrop-shaped pendant. In the center was a beautiful, egg-shaped reddish-brown speckled jasper stone. The metalwork around the stone had been formed into flames.

I looked up at Celeste, who had her hands folded in front of her chest, a soft smile on her face.

"Are these the elemental amulets Pops found in Europe?" I asked.

She smiled a little wider and nodded. "Yes, they are. Raymond always said the energy they put off was familiar, but he never knew how to explain it. I think I know why they felt familiar to him." She paused. "I think they are meant for you."

My brows shot up. "Why would they be meant for us? No one in our bloodline has had elemental power. How would someone have known to make them for us?"

She reached into the box to pull out the last one and carefully unwrapped it. "According to the legend of these amulets, the maker could supposedly see the future. His notes stated that the amulets would strengthen the elemental powers of the firstborn daughters of two siblings who didn't have paranormal powers but were from a paranormal bloodline."

I stared at her for a few moments, trying to figure out what she meant. "I still don't understand what that has to do with us."

She chuckled softly. "Elliott and Sylvia are the first in your bloodline who didn't get powers. You and Izzy are their firstborn daughters. According to the legend, these daughters would have all five of the elemental powers. These pendants should strengthen them."

My eyes grew wider and wider as I processed her words. I glanced at Izzy, who paled visibly. Colin must have noticed because he wrapped his arms around her to steady her.

Luca came up beside me and moved the ringlet that had fallen into my eyes. "Are you okay?" he asked.

I nodded and tried to find my voice. "Did Pops know about any of this?"

Celeste's brow rose. "I mentioned something to him when you two first started showing signs of elemental powers, but he said didn't think you would each have all five. He wasn't sure you would ever gain all five between the two of you either. It is very rare."

I tried to take slow and steady breaths. "Do you know how these stones are supposed to enhance our powers?"

"I'm sorry. The legend doesn't explain anything about how they work. You're welcome to take the files and amulets home to read more about them." She gently placed her hand on my arm. "Just have the receptionist call me when you're finished here, and I'll bring it down to you."

Izzy and I nodded, and she headed back toward the hall. I carefully rewrapped the fire amulet, and Izzy wrapped the spirit amulet Celeste had handed her. We put them back into the box, and I tucked them into the pocket of my bag.

We finished with the doctor and made sure we hadn't left anything behind.

Izzy

We grabbed dinner on the way home, and after we ate, Luca and Colin slumped down onto the love seat as Sadie and I took the couch.

Sadie pulled the box of amulets out of her bag and slid it closer to me. She unwrapped each of the amulets and laid them on top of their cloth wrapping. "So, these are the amulets we read about in Pops's diary. I figured they would be much bigger. These are smaller than a quarter."

I nodded and picked up the air element amulet. I held it up to get a better look at the stone. "Pops's diary said he wasn't sure what type of stone this was. It looks like it might be blue lace agate, which is very rare. I have a few small pieces, but mine don't have all the translucent layers with the white bands. It makes it look like actual clouds."

Sadie looked at me, her wide eyes filled with curiosity. "Wow, I didn't realize you knew so much about the gemstones and stuff."

My brows creased and my eyes narrowed when I tried to recall where I learned that. "I don't know how I know that actually." I shrugged and laid it back into the box. "Do you really think these were made for us? It's hard to believe that someone wrote a prophecy about us."

Sadie nodded and pulled the file from her bag. She opened it and laid it on the table so we could both see it. Most of the pages were in a different language, but we found a couple of pages that looked as if they had been translated. After reading them, Sadie and I shared a look.

"Okay, this says exactly what Celeste told us. But how do we use them?"

I shrugged and peered into the box. "Maybe we just have to have them in our possession. They might work like the pocket stones I charge."

She turned to the guys. "Do either of you have anything to add?"

Colin met my gaze. "Nope. Sounds like you two are on the right track."

I stared at the amulets. "So, I guess you can take the fire and water, and I'll take the air one and the earth one until you need them."

She pointed to the spirit amulet. "What do we do with this one?"

"We should probably carry it on us and see if anything happens," I said.

Sadie took the amulets from me, but I could tell she was contemplating something. "I see your gears turning. What are you thinking about?"

She shook her head and looked at Luca and Colin. "I didn't realize this earlier, but when I have my premonitions, sometimes I can see things playing before me like a movie, but other times, it's just an image like I'm looking at a photo." She sighed. "When I had the premonition about drawing the sigil into the herbs, it was like I was watching it in black and white. The rest of them have been in color."

Luca quickly sat up. "So, it was like you were watching a witch in an old black-and-white film standing at a cauldron while she drew it in the herbs?"

Sadie nodded, but her nose scrunched, and she tilted her head. "Yeah, but it's like I saw her doing it as if I were doing it myself. From my own perspective."

Colin jerked up and made eye contact with Luca. He closed his eyes and took a deep breath before letting it out. "If you're seeing it as if you were doing the sigil and it was in black and white, it means you're seeing memories of your ancestors from your particular bloodline."

Sadie looked at me then back at Luca and Colin. "I'm going to assume by your reaction that it's either a bad thing or its very rare."

Luca reached for her hand, and she gave it to him.

"This is very rare," he said, "and as far as that particular premonition, it wasn't bad."

Sadie stared at him as if waiting for more of an explanation.

He rubbed his thumb over the back of her hand. "It's been rumored that powerful paranormals have had the ability to continue their evil deeds through premonitions to their descendants."

She shook her head. "So, what does that mean exactly?"

"It means that you'll have to figure out if you can trust your black-and-white premonitions. I'll use Hazel Craig as an example. When she first wrote her spells, she was on the side of good. As time went on, evil took over. So, you would have to figure out what version of Hazel was in the premonition."

Sadie let out a little growl and leaned back on the couch as she covered her face. After a moment, she slammed her hands down beside her and looked at the guys. "Someone at the GWP needs to make a collection of memories to upload into our brains. It needs to be step-by-step instructions on how to live this type of life and specifically contain a troubleshooting section."

Luca shot Sadie a toothy grin and chuckled. "They have something similar. It's called the Paranormal Archives."

She rolled her eyes at him. "And just how long would it take to get through all of them?"

His grin turned sheepish. "Only three lifetimes."

She reached behind her, grabbed a pillow, and flung it at him, hitting him square in the chest. Luca made a little huff and gasped for air. He gave her a blank expression then lunged toward her and started tickling her.

Chapter Twenty-Nine

Saturday, July 8, 2023

Sadie

I sat at the dining room table with Luca, a stale doughnut in front of me that I had stuck six birthday candles in and lit only one. Holding my hand about three inches in front of the flame, I flicked my finger toward the next candle, lighting it.

Luca stared at the flame and cleared his throat. "Um. Is that all you can do? *Flick* the flame?"

I furrowed my brows and looked at him then the candles. "Well, kinda. Is that not good progress?" I turned to see his reaction.

His face bore no emotion, but he quickly shrugged. "Yeah. I guess it's better than when you couldn't do it at all."

I clapped my hands like a child would when given praise, and Luca slowly turned to me. I couldn't hold back my giggles anymore. I grabbed the flame between my fingers, held it in front of us, then flicked it toward the holder on the other side of the table with a regular tall, skinny candle.

His eyes went wide, and he huffed. "Well. That is pretty impressive." He turned to me, and the edges of his mouth lifted. "What else have ya got?"

I shrugged trying to play off my excitement. "As long as a flame is within ten feet of me, I can turn it into a fireball and shoot it about fifty yards and almost hit my target."

"Well, Miss Sadie. Color me impressed. I'm proud of you. I know it must have been tough trying to learn all this stuff without my help."

I caught his magnetic gaze. He licked his lips, reached up to gently lift my chin, and pressed his mouth to mine, kissing me like I'd been away for months. I kissed him back hard, trying to let him know how much I missed him while he was asleep.

After a few moments, he pulled back, capturing my gaze again. Reaching up, he wiped the tear that I hadn't realized was sneaking down my cheek. I gave him a small smile. I quickly waved my hand then closed it into a fist, extinguishing the candle flames.

Luca blinked a couple of times, looking from the candles to me. "Well, I've never seen anyone put candles out like that before."

I shot him a smirk. "I wanted to stand out."

He reached up and lifted my chin again. "Sadie, you can be in a roomful of people, and your beauty would stand out above all the rest."

Heat rose into my cheeks. "I hope you mean that. I think you stand out in the crowd too. You're drop-dead gorgeous to me."

A smile crept across his lips. "I guess we were *simply meant to be*."

Luca nodded, and as he went to stand, he paused and tilted his head. "Do you hear that?"

Izzy

I finished showing Colin what I could do with my air and earth element powers and told him what I'd been able to do at the arena.

He listened to me like a boy listening to a story about a super-hero. "Well, it sounds like you have everything down except the strength behind it. We can definitely work on that." He reached around to scratch a spot on his back, but couldn't seem to find it. "Ugh. I have no clue what is on my fur, but it's stiff, and I can feel it on my skin. It's driving me crazy."

My eyes widened, and I glanced away as heat rose in my cheeks.

Colin put his hand on mine. "Why do I get the feeling you know what it is?"

I gave a quick nod but didn't look up. "It's salt water."

"What do you mean it's salt water?" he asked in confusion.

I tilted my head toward my shoulder and shrugged while playing with the obsidian stone in my hand. "Well, you were asleep, and I missed you and was scared. I held you every time we came to visit, so I may or may not have cried all over your fur."

He chuckled and pulled me closer to him on the couch. "Oh, sunshine. It's okay."

I tried to hold back the tears because I knew he didn't like to be touched. "Are you sure you're not mad at me for picking you up?"

His brows furrowed. "Given the circumstances, no, I'm not mad. I probably wouldn't be mad even if you pet me on a normal day." He squirmed a little, rubbing his back against the couch. "I do have a favor to ask of you, though."

My eyes widened as I held his gaze. "Of course. Anything." He scrunched his face. "I don't mind that it's your tears in my fur, but can you please brush it so it's not stiff anymore?"

My brow shot up in surprise. "You want me to brush your fur?"

He nodded and jumped up off the couch to grab his duffel bag from the foyer, then came back to the couch and started to dig through the side pocket. After a moment of searching, he pulled out a metal comb and dropped his bag to the floor. "Are you sure you don't mind?"

I shook my head, trying not to get too excited about him letting me brush him. Him trusting me with his beautiful fur coat warmed my heart. I accepted the comb, and his spiritual cloud wrapped around him, revealing Smokey as it dissipated.

He turned his back toward me and sat on his haunches. "*The stiff spots are between my shoulder blades and halfway down my back.*"

I took a deep breath and slowly let it out as I got into a better position, then I gently placed my hand between his shoulder blades to find the spot. I didn't feel anything on the surface of his fur, so I figured it must be at his skin. I carefully ran the comb through the spot, trying not to pull if I found the stiff part. I ran the comb down a few more times, going farther with each stroke. As I lifted the comb to make another pass, the fur on his back rippled.

"*Can you tell if I got it?*" I ran my fingers through the area.

He squirmed a little, as if trying to feel that particular area. "*I think you did on that one.*"

I combed the section again, watching his fur ripple. Then I continued down his back with my hand, following the stroke of the comb so I didn't miss any spots.

I ran the comb over his side, still catching some of his back. He made a weird groaning sound and repositioned. I waited a moment then continued down both sides. About fifteen seconds into it, I noticed he was making a weird rumbling sound, and I stopped.

"*Um. Smokey. Are you purring?*" I asked.

He jerked his head toward me. "*I don't think so. I've never purred before. I don't think I can.*"

I reached up and scratched both sides of his face and under his chin. He leaned into my hands more, and I deepened the scratch up and down the sides of his neck and chin. Pursing his lips when I got to his cheeks.

His eyes rolled back. "*Okay, I take it back. Maybe I can purr.*"

I smiled and moved slowly down the sides of his body, making circles in his fur. He stretched and stood on his back tippy-toes, alternating his paws. He made the noise again, and it sounded like a rusty engine starting up.

"*I think you need to be oiled. You sound a little rusty.*"

He looked up at me with narrowed eyes. "*My cat body is over a hundred years old, and I've never had a reason to purr. What did you think it would sound like? To be honest, I didn't even know I could purr.*"

A giggle slipped from me as Luca came into the room with Sadie right behind him.

Luca looked around for a moment before his eyes stopped on me and Smokey, and he straightened. "Dude. Are you purring?" he asked, his expression filled with confusion.

"*So what if I am? Are you jealous, Luca?*" Smokey mumbled.

Luca reached up and rubbed the sides of his head. "Dude, you are getting so soft."

Smokey turned to him, stepping out of my reach. "*You should try it. Maybe you would be less grumpy all the time.*"

Luca shook his head. "Nah. I'll pass. We're going to watch a movie. If you stay in that form, you need to stop purring. It's kinda creepy."

Smokey rolled his eyes, and his spiritual cloud formed around him again, revealing Colin as it dissipated. He leaned over and kissed my cheek. "Thank you, sunshine. I feel much better."

Chapter Thirty

Thursday, July 14, 2023

Sadie

The last week went by in a blur. Izzy, Colin, Luca, and I were at the shop during the day then at the arena from six to nine every night. The GWP still hadn't found a way to close the rift for good, so Luca and Colin were working with us to strengthen our energy blasts and elemental powers.

Word had gotten around about the sigil pendant that Izzy had made, and she ended up getting orders for twenty-three more from the GWP members who would be helping fight Tobias. Barnaby had even come by to order an obsidian pocket stone for protection with a sigil for stamina. He would be helping his sister, Mavis, and a few others keep the wards going as well as the glamour spell to make the area look empty.

We hadn't received any updates from Cyrus in the past week, which had left Neva worried. She was doing her best to stay busy at the GWP searching for a way to close the rift.

Mel and Donald had been helping Tyson get everything from the Demorian grimoire into the database.

According to Izzy's last blink, and the GWP's calculations of Demoria's lunar cycle compared to ours, tomorrow would be the day that Tobias was supposed to come into our realm to get the spell book and bring his people here.

The paranormals raised wards and put up glamours all over town to protect the locals from seeing or being injured by Tobias and his men.

We didn't know how Cyrus would be when he came back, but we assumed Tobias would have some type of controlling spell on Cyrus to keep him loyal.

Celeste made some potions from the Demorian grimoire that we could possibly need for any situation that may arise during his time in our realm. From what the GWP had learned over the last week, we needed to get the amulet away from Tobias and destroy it to have any chance against taking him and his men down. The amulet would still be drawing power from his realm until we broke the connection.

Izzy and I were trying to finish the last of the stones and remedies to be picked up that afternoon when the bell above the door alerted us to someone entering.

Celeste smiled and held up a small white box. "I have something for you all."

As she made her way to the counter, I peeked into the kitchen to let Izzy, Colin, and Luca know she was here. They all stopped what they were doing and came into the front room.

"Hello, everyone," she said in her beautiful Scottish accent. "I have your earpieces for you. I didn't want to wait until tomorrow morning to do everything before Tobias shows up."

Luca nodded and took the box from her. "Thank you, Celeste. How is everyone doing? I know it's been quite a few years since we've faced a threat here in Salem."

Her face went still. "Everyone is nervous. I think it's mainly because we've never fought anyone from another realm like this, especially not a demon."

Colin raised his brows. "No. Not a demon, but they have fought off every other type of monster that has attacked. I have faith that we'll defeat him just like the other monsters we've gone up against."

Celeste shrugged. "You have a point, Colin. I'll mention that when we get the rift sensors signal that Tobias will be arriving soon. I'll be watching the cameras and reporting his locations in your earpieces as he goes."

We all gave a nod.

"I'll let you guys finish up here and see you in the morning. Please get lots of rest. You'll need it." She gave us a small smile and turned to leave.

Colin followed her up front to lock the door behind her. Luca taped the sign to the door stating that we would be closed Friday but we would be at the park if anyone needed an emergency remedy.

Chapter Thirty-One
Friday, July 15, 2023

Izzy

"Daisy. It's time to wake up."

The voice caught me off guard, and I jerked awake. It took a couple of seconds for my eyes to adjust to my surroundings. I stood on Main Street in front of the alleyway and turned to see who was with me. I gasped as I saw Pops leaning against the side of the Bean & Bake. "Oh my gosh. Pops. I've missed you so much." I ran up to him and wrapped him in a hug.

The feeling of being in the veil with Pops was so different from being in Demoria. In the veil, I could actually see my body and feel my surroundings, unlike in Demoria, where I was just a pair of eyes to myself. It was as if I was invisible there, which wasn't a bad thing.

"Hello, Daisy. How are you and Sadie doing?" he asked with a gentle smile.

I shrugged. "Okay, considering what is going to happen tomorrow. We aren't sure if we will be able to get the amulet from Tobias so that he doesn't have his powers."

He handed me a piece of paper. I opened it and saw a spell written in his handwriting.

"Pops. I don't understand. What is this? How did you get it?"

He put his hand on my shoulder. "Daisy, that is almost two months of life in the veil. I've explained my story to dozens of people in here, and each one sent me to see someone else until I met the celestial wizard who helped me write that."

I glanced over the incantation, and my eyes widened. "Is this to close the rift?"

He gave a toothy grin. "Yes, Daisy. That's exactly what that is. You must take this to Celeste, and she will know exactly who should perform this spell. You must wait until Tobias comes into your realm before you close it. If not, he will just open the rift again in twenty-one years. He is the only one powerful enough to open the rift from the inside."

My brows furrowed. "Why is he the only one who can open it? Don't all the demons in that realm have the same powers?"

He gave a curt nod. "They do, but Tobias has made some altercations to himself to where he has implanted some of the amulet power into himself. The power in their realm is dying, so forty-five years ago, he cut open his arm and implanted a piece of their power stone. It takes a while to charge, but the amulet gives him immense power as long as that rift stays open. That realm won't last another twenty-one years for someone else to implant themselves."

I let out a heavy sigh. "So, I guess he's Demoria's version of Ironman. Except he has an amulet instead of a fusion reactor."

Pops chuckled. "Yeah, I guess that's one way to look at it."

"Will he know we closed the rift?" I asked, thinking about how close he could be to us before they shut it.

Pops shook his head. "No. He won't be able to feel it since his body is charged with it. He won't know until he tries to use it."

"We're supposed to be at the Salem Park working on spells from the glamoured Hazel Craig book when he comes through the rift."

Pops smiled. "They will have it closed before he gets there."

I gave him a quick stare down. "Speaking of Hazel Craig's spell book, can you just tell me now where you hid it?"

He smirked. "Well, I could I suppose."

I waited a moment before letting out a sigh. "But you won't because it would mean that you wasted time doing all the puzzles and codes with us as kids, right?"

He raised his hand and placed it on the side of my face, and I leaned into it. "It's not safe for you girls to know where it is. I'll place another hint for you to follow soon."

My eyebrows shot up. "Another hint? You've been giving us hints?"

He gave me a small nod. "I have. Did you really think a black spider would have a green shimmer under the right lighting?"

I thought about it for a moment, remembering what had caught my attention with Charlotte and rubbed my temples. "I can't believe I didn't realize that was your energy color. It makes sense now. You did that so I would remember that story. You planned every single thing out from the time we were born, didn't you?"

He tilted his head toward his shoulder and shrugged. "Well, since your parents told me they were pregnant with you and Sadie. Everything you will ever need to know is in that beautiful brain of yours. And the same goes for Sadie."

I looked down at the bunny charm that Pops had given me this past Easter during our visit. "How do we find it in there, though?"

He pulled me to his side. "You will need to learn to channel it. It will come to you when you really need it. You just have to believe in yourselves." He kissed the top of my head. "You need to get back to your bed now and get that spell to Celeste."

I nodded and wrapped Pops in the biggest hug I could. "We miss you so much, Pops. I love you. And please be safe meeting all of these people in here."

He ran his hand gently over my eyes like he did when I was little to get me to go to sleep. "I love you, too, Daisy. Give Sadie my love."

I slowly opened my eyes, and I was back in my room. "I will," I whispered, hoping he would hear me.

I took a deep breath and slowly let it out then woke Smokey and went to wake Sadie and Binx.

We all met in the living room, and I handed Sadie the paper Pops gave me.

She gasped and ran her fingers over it. "This is Pops's handwriting. Did you blink into the veil again?"

I gave her a small smile and nodded. "He said he loves and misses you too."

She wiped a tear that tried to sneak down her cheek. "Is this a spell to close the rift?"

My chest tightened as I thought about all the work Pops had done for us. "It is." I filled Sadie, Luca, and Colin in on what he'd said as we headed to see Celeste.

Chapter Thirty-Two

Friday, July 15, 2023

Sadie

We got a message from Cyrus's raven this morning. About an hour later, the sensor that Dad and Elijah had made sent us the signal that they were an hour and a half away. Cyrus mentioned that Tobias would, in fact, be putting him under a spell. Because the spell would be from Demoria, he wouldn't be able to see any of our glamours.

We got into position, and the groups of paranormals started putting up their glamours. Salem would look empty to Tobias when he came through, and the people of Salem would not be able to see him either. Protection wards were raised as well. The ten strongest paranormals in Salem lined up in the alleyway entrance beside the Bean & Bake, waiting on Celeste to give the order to close the rift.

When Tobias, Cyrus, and his minions arrived at the park, they would be able to see us but not the half dozen paranormals surrounding us behind the glamours and wards. Colin and Luca stood watch about five feet away behind the glamours. Seeing all those powerful, well-trained paranormals by our side helped ease our worries.

The countdown had begun, and we had thirty minutes before they reached the rift. Celeste started her speech through our earpieces, trying to calm everyone's worries and inspire their courage. She repeated Colin's words from the night before, giving him credit for them. I could picture her standing behind Tyson in the tech room, watching all the monitors, ready to pass out instructions. She was definitely in the right position at the GWP. She was a powerful woman and even supportive and loving when necessary, and she was well respected.

I wished I had her confidence. I was trying to be strong for Izzy, but deep down, I was terrified. Two months ago, our lives were so different. This was not what I would have thought living in Salem would be like. The GWP would be there as backup, but it was up to us to try taking him down first. I had no idea what would happen if things went sideways.

Celeste came across the earpiece. "They are through the rift and on our side. They turned left and are approaching Roots & Remedies."

I turned to Izzy. "I assume Cyrus will have to read that sign to them. I doubt they can read our language, even if they speak it."

She nodded, agreeing with me.

"They are leaving Roots & Remedies, and Cyrus is leading them toward the park," Celeste announced.

Izzy and I pulled the glamoured spell book out of the warded box and flipped it open. The inside of the book was full of what seemed to be stories of werewolves, vampires, witches, wizards, and other traditionally scary beings.

I whispered to Izzy, "I wanna read this when this is all said and done. It looks interesting."

Izzy rolled her eyes and smiled as she started pulling out the herbs, mortar and pestle, and the stones and metals we brought. "Only you would think that."

I shrugged and moved so we were facing each other on the blanket spread beneath us. I laid the book down to the side, away from where Tobias would be approaching so he would think we didn't know he was there.

"Okay. Start closing that rift," Celeste ordered.

"Izzy?" Tyson's voice came across the earpiece. "You did mention that his people would be ready to go, right?"

Her eyebrows furrowed. "Yeah. Why?"

"Well, I've got forty more signatures that just came into range on the sensors," Tyson said.

Izzy sat up straight and tapped her earpiece so everyone could hear her. "Don't worry. We've got this. Tobias will be in custody before they get to the rift." She tapped her earpiece again.

I stared at her.

"What?" she asked.

"I'm trying to believe that we've got this under control, but how on earth are you so sure?" I asked, trying to catch her gaze.

She shrugged. "I believe in Pops, and I believe in this town and the members of the GWP. And most of all, I believe in us."

I smiled. "Look at little Daisy. So brave these days."

She rolled her eyes and nudged me. "What did you expect?"

"Not this. This is the last thing I thought would happen with you two months ago. Now, nothing is too far out of the realm of possibility with you."

She shrugged again. "Maybe not. But let's focus on keeping those Viking-looking people in their own realm."

Her comment brought me back to the present a lot faster than I wanted.

"Sadie, Izzy, they are about two minutes away. Keep your powers a secret as long as you can," Celeste announced.

Izzy and I took a deep breath and pretended to be mixing a spell from the book. Izzy added the herbs, and I crushed them with the pestle.

Another voice came across the earpiece. "We're about halfway done closing this rift. We need five more minutes." "Girls, hold him off as long as you can," Celeste ordered.

I looked around at the paranormals surrounding us, and they nodded as we made eye contact. When I glanced at Luca, he gestured to the book and winked.

"*They're here,*" Luca said telepathically, raising goose bumps along my spine.

I whispered to Izzy, "Here we go."

We continued working on the mixture, and I waved my hands over the pestle as if to activate it. I waited a moment before throwing my hands up in defeat as if the spell had failed.

"He's just watching you two. Try again."

Luca walked to where we could see him without looking up, and Colin stepped up beside him. They both squatted down.

Frowning at the book, I flipped back a page. "I don't know what we did wrong. That one should have worked," I said to Izzy, not knowing if Tobias could hear us or not.

She sat up and shook out her shoulders and arms. "Let's try it again. We are the Craig bloodline. We have powers in us somewhere."

I gave Izzy a quick nod and pretended to try again.

"They are stepping closer but trying to stay hidden. I think they want to listen to you for a few minutes," Colin said telepathically to me.

I glanced up at him since I was unaware that he could do that. Realizing what I was doing, I pretended to sneeze.

Izzy acted startled for a moment. "Bless you. A little warning next time. You scared me with that sneeze."

I scrunched my nose. "Sorry, you know how my allergies are. I wish these spells could be done inside."

Izzy shrugged. "Well, we don't wanna catch the house on fire. Where else would we try to do spells?"

"Tobias is approaching now. He's about forty feet away. Thirty, now twenty. I think he's staying there. Keep going," Luca announced.

"Izzy, do you think we'll ever get the hang of this? I mean, our parents don't have powers, so maybe we didn't get them either," I said, sounding defeated. I waved my hands over the mortar again then growled "See? I don't think we have them."

"Maybe I could help you two ladies with that," Tobias said louder than necessary.

Izzy and I jumped and turned toward him, trying to hide the spell book. "Oh no. You don't have to help us with anything, sir. We are just practicing our lines for a Halloween play we are in for the festival in a few months," I said, trying to buy the paranormals more time to close the rift.

He shook his head and took a step closer, his two minions following on the left side of him and Cyrus on his right. Cyrus stared at us with black eyes as if he was ready to pounce when Tobias gave the order. Tobias raised his hand, forming a fist. A spark of his power shot toward us. Izzy and I dropped to the ground pretending to be helpless.

"Did we do something wrong, mister?" Izzy asked with a convincingly shaky voice.

He nodded and raised his fist again, shooting another spark. This time, it hit the protection wards and slid to the ground. His eyes turned solid black, and Izzy and I got to our feet.

He turned to his minions. "Get that book," he demanded.

They started to approach and stopped suddenly as if they had hit a glass wall. They backed up and hit the ward with sparks of their energy. Every consecutive one they shot seemed a little less powerful. Izzy and I flinched every time they hit the ward.

Tobias raised his fist. "That old man must have put a protection spell on them. Keep shooting."

Cyrus stood waiting for orders and staring us down. Tobias and his minions shot at the ward another few moments, then Tobias walked forward with his hand out in front of him, feeling for the ward.

A woman's voice came over our earpieces. "Almost there." A few seconds passed. "It's closed. Take that demon down."

I glanced at Cyrus, who seemed to be trying to figure out where he was. He shook his head then looked at me, gave a half smile, and winked. That was the signal he said he would give to let us know it was him. I nudged Izzy, and when she glanced at him, he winked again. She let out a breath she seemed to have been holding.

Tobias turned to his minions. "Why are you just standing there? Shoot." He turned toward Cyrus. "You, get me that book."

Cyrus stalked toward us as if to attack. About five feet away, he turned and shot an energy ball at Tobias, who stumbled back as it struck his chest. One of his minions helped keep him upright.

"Get off me, and go get me that book!" Tobias screamed.

"But, sir, our powers aren't working," the one to his right exclaimed.

"You two are useless. Get out of my way!" Tobias shoved the closest one and raised both hands. He curled them into fists, trying to shoot sparks toward the wards, then looked at Cyrus. "What did you do?"

Cyrus smiled. "Who me? I did what I was supposed to do—pretend to be on your side. I think I did that very well." He rushed to Luca, grabbed an earpiece, and turned it on. "See, buttercup? I told you I'd be okay."

Neva's voice came across the earpiece. "Yes, you did, baby. Now take that monster into custody."

Tobias stormed toward Cyrus. I called upon my powers and formed the biggest energy ball I could, then sent it toward Tobias, hitting him square in the chest. He fell back, and his head slammed into the ground. Izzy shot both of his minions with energy balls, one from each hand, causing them to fly backward and slam onto their backs. Luca and Colin stepped out from behind the glamour and approached them, ready to fire their own energy balls if the minions tried to move.

I nodded to Luca and Colin, and they gave the order to lower the glamours.

As Tobias got to his feet, he slowly scanned the area, stopping when he got to me and Izzy. "That old man said you two didn't have powers, and so did my informant."

Izzy shrugged. "You didn't really think you could come here and kill two of our people and actually get the truth out of anybody, did you?"

Tobias charged me, grabbing me before I could form an energy ball. We fell to the ground, and he rolled onto his back, pulling me closer to him and holding a knife to my side. "Give me the book, or I'll kill her. I'm done playing games with you mortals."

He scrambled up, dragging me to my feet.

"*Don't let anyone move. I've got this,*" I said to Luca.

He raised his hand, keeping everyone in their places.

Slowly reaching into my pocket, I found the potion stashed there that I wanted to try. I'd had a black-and-white premonition a few nights before and made it without telling Luca. I wasn't sure what book I'd been looking at in my premonition, but it was a spell for bottling a flame.

I gently popped the cork and poured the mixture on the side of Tobias's pants where they covered his boots and weren't touching his skin. Tobias was still yelling demands at Luca and Colin, and Izzy was slowly walking to grab the fake spell book.

I whispered the incantation and snapped my fingers, causing a small flame to start on the side of his pants. Luca's eyes shot open, and he cleared his throat. He covered his mouth to hide the smile forming there. I glanced down at the flame as it started creeping up his leg.

Reaching back into my pocket, I grabbed the auto-injecting syringe Tyson had given me. He had informed me that it was the same type they would shoot an approaching Lycan with. They used to put a tranquilizing serum in them, but I had made the same sleeping potion from the Demorian grimoire that Maggie had given Luca and Colin.

I lowered my hand toward the flames on his pants and flicked some of the flame onto the ground. A few moments later, one of his minions had noticed his pants on fire. He got Tobias's attention and pointed to his pants, and when Tobias looked down at his leg, he pushed me toward the ground, dropping his knife. I faked a gasp as he tried to smack the flames out. While he was distracted,

I quickly plunged the needle into his calf. After a few seconds, I closed my fist, extinguishing the flames.

I stood quickly, backing away from Tobias and signaling to Izzy that I had given him the potion. Tobias balled up his fist and attempted to shoot a spark of energy at me.

I smiled. "What's wrong, Tobias? Is your power not working?"

Rage filled his face, and he balled both fists to try again. This time, a spark came barreling out of his fists but fell short of hitting me. "What did you guys do?" He looked at his minions again. "I thought I told you two to get these wards down and get me that book."

His minions just stared at him, not wanting to risk the pain of an energy ball from Luca or Colin.

"Just give up, Tobias. You don't have any power here," Cyrus called out.

Tobias undid the top few buttons of his shirt and reached inside to pull his empty hand back out and show it to us. Suddenly, he lowered his right hand from under the edge of his jacket to reveal a small knife. He threw it at me, and the blade landed in my left thigh. I fell to my knees, clutching the knife as I pulled it out. I made eye contact with Izzy, and she started chanting the incantation to the potion I'd injected Tobias with. After a few moments, Tobias fell to the ground. His minions quickly sat up and raised their hands in surrender.

Cyrus and Colin bound the two minions, and Luca came over to tend to my wound. He wrapped his belt around my thigh to stop the bleeding and ripped off a piece of the blanket we had been sitting on to tie it around my thigh over the cut.

Static sounded in my earpiece, making me jump. "Luca, bring her straight to the medical ward. Cyrus and Colin, the transport wagon is on its way."

I laid my head against Luca's chest, trying to ignore my pain as I closed my eyes and listened to his heartbeat on our way the GWP. I should have felt more relaxed now that Tobias was in custody, but my gut told me it wasn't over yet.

Izzy

Cyrus transported Tobias and his minions from the park to the GWP without incident.

As Colin and I headed to the medical ward to check on Sadie, the lead paranormal at the rift spoke across the earpiece. "The rift is opening again. I think the people on the other side are holding it open somehow. We need help over here."

Colin and I took off running to Main Street. As we turned the corner, about halfway down the street, we saw small sparks of energy coming through the rift. When we got to the alley, the rift looked like a bolt of lightning opening at its center. Every ten seconds, a larger spark of energy burst through.

I walked around the group of paranormals surrounding the rift. A breeze had started when we were at the park, so I wanted to use that to my advantage.

"I have an idea," I said, loud enough so everyone could hear. "When I say so, I want you guys to release the rift and allow it to open just a bit more. I'll blast them away from the rift on the other side. Colin..." I met his gaze. "I'm gonna need a major boost when I release."

The sides of his mouth turned up, and he got into position. "Let me know when you're ready, sunshine."

I stood back far enough that the larger sparks coming through wouldn't hit me then raised my hand to get a better feel for the direction of the breeze. I took a deep breath and allowed the wind to flow through me, charging my power. I started pulling at the breeze, drawing it to my body as if I were holding a large pile of laundry. Once I felt like I couldn't hold anymore, I squeezed the air tighter to condense it and added more as the breeze blew around me. After about a minute, I held my arms tight and gripped the clouded ball in between my palms.

"Okay. Release the rift in three... two... one..."

The paranormals took a step back, and Colin moved behind me, placing his hands on my shoulders. His battery power poured into me. I took a deep breath while I siphoned as much of his energy as I could. Once the rift opened far enough to fit a basketball through, I pushed the clouded ball of air into the rift. A moment later, the sparks stopped, and low screams slipped through the opening.

"Close it now!" I shouted, and the paranormals all gathered around once more, forcing their energies into the rift, quickly closing it. After about fifteen seconds, the lightning bolt was closed in the center and started shrinking. Once it got down to about half an inch tall, a bubble-type spark formed and popped.

We all released a sigh of relief.

The head paranormal turned to me. "Thank you so much. We couldn't have done this without you, Izzy."

I smiled and leaned against Colin. "I'm glad I could help."

Colin and I headed back to the GWP while we listened to them report back to Celeste on the earpiece that the rift was completely closed. She told them that another group would come relieve them so they could rest. The rift location would be monitored by members of the GWP for the next few weeks for any activity, while my dad and Elliott worked on the sensor.

I took Colin's hand, and he smiled down at me.

"I am so proud of you, sunshine. You took charge of the situation, and you were successful. The GWP will probably use the video footage for familiar training, with your permission, of course."

I put my head on his arm as heat rose in my cheeks. "Thank you for boosting me."

He stopped me and lifted my chin, forcing me to look at him. "Anything for you, sunshine," he said, leaning down and kissing me.

My heart fluttered, and he pulled away, wrapping his arm around me.

I leaned into him and hooked my thumb in the back pocket of his jeans. "Let's go check on Sadie."

Chapter Thirty-Three

Friday, July 15, 2023

Sadie

I woke a couple of hours later, and the pain in my leg had subsided. I had given the doctor some of the healing salve as a thank-you for taking care of Binx and Smokey while they were under that Demorian sleeping potion.

Luca, Colin, Izzy, Celeste, Neva, Cyrus, and Mel all stood around the bed as I realized where I was.

When Celeste saw I was awake, she sat on the bed beside me and took my hand in hers. "I am very impressed with that little fire trick you pulled. How did you know how to do that?"

I smiled, pushing myself into a sitting position. "I had a premonition. A black-and-white one, and I was looking at the page of a very old book."

Celeste glanced at Luca and Colin then back at me. "It seems as if your ancestor Hazel Craig was trying to help you."

My brows furrowed in confusion. "What do you mean? How do you know these visions are coming from her?"

"One of the spells in her spell book is for bottling the elements, but that spell is one she wrote before she was taken over by evil. It is said that a second spell book exists that had a lot of those same spells but were all used for good. It has been lost over the centuries, but it seems as if she is helping you from beyond the grave and showing you those spells."

I twisted a strand of hair around my finger as I thought back to my premonitions. "So, was the premonition about the sigil in the salve one from that book too?"

Celeste nodded. "We believe so."

I peered up at Celeste. "But why show me these spells now?"

She looked at Izzy then me. "That we aren't sure of, but every power the two of you have gotten, she had. We assume that she is showing you because you guys remind her of her former self, before the evil took over."

"Do you think she will show me spells from the evil one?" I looked down at my hands.

Celeste shrugged. "I'm not sure, but you'll know just by the ingredients and words of the spells."

I gave her a quick nod and scanned the people in the room. "Are Tobias and his minions behind bars?"

Cyrus nodded. "Yes. Thanks to you administering that sleeping potion."

I met Celeste's eyes and sat up straighter. "I wanna see him."

She nodded and reached into her pocket, pulling out a syringe of the same color potion that we had given Binx and Smokey. "We figured you would want to wake him. But I want Luca and Colin to go with you and Izzy."

I carefully walked down to the cells, refusing Luca's help. The area was not what I had expected. No doors consisting of vertical bars caged them in. Instead, each cell was a white room with an observation window and a heavy steel door. The first room held one of Tobias's minions, who was being interrogated by Paxton. For a split second, I felt bad for him, but then I remembered what he had come here to do, and the feeling passed quicker than it came.

I avoided looking into the rest of the cells as we passed.

Celeste turned down a little hallway and stopped at the observation window of the last cell. "Tobias is in here," she said as she waved to a security guard at the end of the small hallway. "Inject the potion then come stand at the door to recite the incantation. I don't know how fast he will come out of the spell."

I nodded, and Izzy walked beside me, holding my arm to steady me as we approached the demon. I pushed the tip of the syringe into his upper arm and watched as it emptied. We quickly backed up, and I stepped out of the room and stood at the window to look in. Izzy said the incantation then stepped aside so the guard could seal the door.

It took a minute for Tobias to wake and sit up.

Celeste gestured to a button to the left of the window. "Push that button once, and it will turn on the speaker."

I pressed the button. "Why do you want this spell book so bad?" I asked, startling Tobias.

Tobias franticly looked around. "Who said that?" he asked as he peeked under his bed.

Celeste waved her hand at the camera, and the light above us came on.

Tobias stared at me through the window as his eyes grew wide. He stood and came to the window. "How did you do that? I couldn't see you a moment ago." His brow furrowed.

Celeste smiled. "It's a one-way mirror. You will only see out of it when we allow it."

He looked at her with rage then jerked his head toward me. "What do you want, child?"

I rolled my eyes at the name. "Why do you want that spell book?"

"Why do you care?" He folded his arms across his chest.

"Did you ever think to ask for our help to transfer your power to our realm? I'm fairly sure the Green Witch Project would have been more than happy to help you."

Tobias dropped his arms and put his hands on the glass. It shocked him, and he jumped back with a growl. "I would never stoop so low as to be nice to the likes of you witches. My people will find a way to this realm, and they will take over and free me."

I shook my head and turned to Izzy.

The corners of her mouth shot up, and she looked straight at Tobias. "The rift is closed and locked for good. At the rate your minion said the power of your world was depleting, no one will have enough power to open it from your realm's side again."

Tobias slowly backed away. "Why did you even ask why I wanted the book if you already knew the answer?"

Izzy shrugged. "We wanted to see if you would tell the truth. Who was your informant inside the GWP?"

His eyes met hers, and his brow shot up in confusion. "What?"

"You told Cyrus your informant said we didn't have any powers," she replied.

Tobias chuckled. "Oh, that. I can sense power. That's why we were coming to your realm. We wanted some of that power. I couldn't sense any on you when I passed you that day outside Roots & Remedies."

My brows raised. "So, no one was feeding you information?"

"No. Like I said earlier, I would never stoop low enough to work with the likes of you."

I smiled at Tobias and hooked my arm in Izzy's. "We will let you get back to looking at the four walls surrounding you. We've wasted enough time with you and your minions the past two months. I hope you enjoy the sound of your own voice, Tobias. It's probably the only one you will hear for quite a while." I pressed the button on the wall beside me to turn off the speaker, and the light above our heads went off.

I turned to Luca and gave him my best puppy-dog eyes and pouty lip. "I surrender. You can carry me now."

He chuckled and scooped me up in his arms to carry me back to the medical ward.

Chapter Thirty-Four

Friday, July 15, 2023

Sadie

We made a quick pit stop at the library to get the book Pops had in the coded note. Since we already had the code to decipher from the first edition, we just needed the new edition. I hobbled back to where I had looked the other day and found it, then took it back up to the librarian to check out.

Luca and Colin made dinner for us as we sat in the dining room with our notes and our codex and started to decipher the same type of code with *A Discovery of Witchcraft*. After about twenty-five minutes, the guys brought in our dinner just as we were finishing the last word. A moment later, I held up the completed puzzle, and we all stared at it.

I let out a low growl and looked up at the ceiling. "Really, Pops, a riddle? You never taught us those."

Not a safe place to hide, but a safe place to seek.

For a sneak peek into Broken Blood Spell, visit the shop on my website for a free download.

www.stacyrae-author.com

Acknowledgments

I would like to thank all my family and friends who have dealt with my book talk and read snippets. Thank you to Marissa and Amanda for doing the beta reads for me. Also, a huge thank you to my editors, Lynn, Jessica, Rashida, Amanda, and Brittany at Red Adept Editing, for helping me through my journey.

A huge thank you goes out to Painted Wings Publishing as well. They did an amazing job on the edges for my special edition of this series as well as the chapter image. If you ordered my book from my website, the paper that was wrapped around the book was also designed by them. They are definitely worth working with, and I look forward to doing my next series with them.

About the Author

I can't believe I've published a second book. Writing Sadie and Izzy's journey has been such an exciting experience. I'm so glad to have my readers joining them.

I have a son from my first marriage and a daughter and two stepsons with my husband. We have four cats and lots of local wildlife that surround us every day. I have incorporated some of the wildlife into this book along with some of our cats, one of which passed away as I began this adventure. Some of my characters are named after close family and friends as well.

I hope this series is one you will enjoy following these girls through. I have definitely enjoyed writing their story.

You can find me on the following social media platforms, through email, and website:

Facebook: Stacy Rae-Author

TikTok: @stacyrae_author

Email me at: stacyrae.author@gmail.com

Website: www.stacyrae-author.com

Also By

All the artwork in this version of *Demon in the Rift* was drawn by Stacy in Procreate. The photo of the sky on the front cover was taken by my husband in Arlington, VA, from his tower crane.

Keep a look out for other titles.

The Familiar Process- Prequel to The Green Witch Project Series

A Spell to Bind- Book One of The Green Witch Project Series

Demon in the Rift- Book Two of *The Green Witch Project Series*

Broken Blood Spell- Book Three of The Green Witch Project Series

Evil Innocence- Book One of the Dreamer's Innocence Series